A Far Away Magic

Praise for *A Girl Called Owl*

'A sparkling, frosty read, full of feisty characters, myth and mystery' *Daily Mail*

'A winter treat full of frosty magic' Katherine Woodfine, bestselling author of *The Mystery of the Clockwork Sparrow*

'A magical debut' *Bookseller*

'Deftly integrates figures from folklore and ancient mythology into the wider narrative of family, friendship and identity' *Primary Times*

'A perfect read for those who love wintry magic and a strong female character proving her place in the world' BookTrust

'An impressive coming-of-age debut novel, *A Girl Called Owl* combines elements of mystery, adventure, romance, fantasy and folklore' SLA

Books by Amy Wilson

A Girl Called Owl

A Far Away Magic

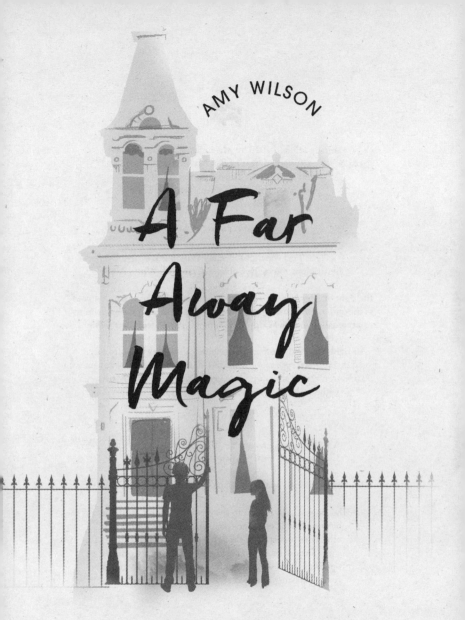

AMY WILSON

A Far Away Magic

Illustrated by Helen Crawford-White

MACMILLAN CHILDREN'S BOOKS

First published 2018 by Macmillan Children's Books
an imprint of Pan Macmillan
20 New Wharf Road, London N1 9RR
Associated companies throughout the world
www.panmacmillan.com

ISBN 978-1-5098-3775-5

1 3 5 7 9 8 6 4 2

A CIP catalogue record for this book is available from
the British Library.

Printed and bound by CPI Group (UK) Ltd, Croydon CR0 4YY

For Matt

I saw them in the skies
In the corners of my eyes
Darkness, shadows, creeping close,
And the boy stood alone, afraid.

I told him he could fight them all
He knew it; he was ten feet tall
Magic in his veins and power in his blood,
He was afraid of himself.

Bavar

There's a massive mirror in the drawing room. It haunts me. If you look hard enough, if you look in just the right way, you can see yourself for who you could be. There is always the hope. Most of the time it just shows me exactly what all the others see; what we all become in this house. The crooked spine, the sallow skin, the dark hair that curls and grows out. Nose is longer, more prominent than an average boy's nose. Shadows cling tight and there's a warp in the air around me.

So, not average.

But in the right light, at the right time of the day and with the right frame of mind, I can see something else. Straighter, brighter – a bit like a normal boy. A bit like hope.

'Bavar!'

In a hopeless house.

'BaVAR!'

Aoife is my aunt, my mother's sister. Her kindness comes in cake form.

'School,' she says, handing me a wicker basket.

I usually leave it beneath the old oak tree at the end of the garden. It's overgrown there, thick with brambles and nettles.

'Will you be back at the usual time, Bavar?'

'Yes.'

'Friends?'

'No.'

She nods, her grey eyes unsmiling. 'Maybe tomorrow.'

'Maybe.'

We have the same conversation every day, and I do the thing with the basket every day. Stuff the ham roll into my jacket pocket along with the wedge of cake. A red apple.

Uncle Sal waves from the study window as I head out. His glasses glint in the sun; he looks more mole-like than ever at a distance.

'Say something,' I tell myself. 'Say something. Tell them about lunchboxes. Crisps. Biscuits. Tell them you don't like beetroot cake; it looks like a bloody pulp by the time you get to school. Tell them –' I hiss to myself, as I wedge the basket next to the withered trunk of the oak, once Uncle Sal has turned from the window – 'there will be no friends; there will be no need for all the cake.'

I know that much at least.

Angel

Idiots, all these people. My first day at the new school, and all the same old idiots wanting to know all the same old rubbish.

I've been lying through my teeth for all of registration. Told one of them my mum was a ballet dancer; told another my dad was in MI5. Said I lived in the massive yellow house on top of the hill that looks over the town. Said I lived in a purple caravan.

They know I'm lying. They won't like me for it. With every turn of my tale, their eyes get narrower, their faces tighter, and it feels good. Satisfying.

'*Why do you do it?*' my mum's voice asks, deep in my head. All soft and sad.

'Because I can. What do you care? You're not here any more,' I reply.

'*I do wish you wouldn't,*' my dad says, his voice a bit more stern, a bit more disappointed.

'Can you wish, where you are?' I answer. 'Because I don't think so.'

And then it's my first English lesson, and a monster walks in. Well. It's a boy, of course. But he looks like a monster. Like a monster who knows he's a monster so he's trying to make himself smaller so nobody else will notice, only in doing that he makes himself more twisted, more monstrous. He shuffles into the classroom, shoulders hunched, chin to his chest, dark curls standing out all round his head. There's a ripple in the air around him as everyone looks away, hurriedly finding a place to sit. They don't even tease him, it's like he's not really there.

Who is THAT?

He sits one row over, one row in front of me, and I watch him for the whole lesson. He's not like anyone I ever saw before. Somehow it's hard to see him clearly, like he's actively deflecting any attempt. It doesn't work on me – I see him. I can see things other people don't see anyway; have done ever since the thing with Mum and Dad.

But I never saw a living, breathing boy like this one.

He never looks up. He grunts when the teacher calls out the register. Bavar. A good name, I reckon. A good name for a boy who looks like that. I stare – I can't help myself. But he doesn't look around, though he must feel me watching him.

He writes with his left hand curled tight over his work, his head bent low. Every so often his shoulders twitch, as if he's been jolted from sleep. I follow him at the end of the day, past all the clusters of kids who don't notice him. He walks with his head down, his feet heavy against the pavement, and I'll be late back if I keep going, but I can't stop myself, because he smells like that night, with Mum and Dad, and there's that same twist in the air around him.

All the things I told myself weren't real, and here he is.

And he's *definitely* real.

'Hey!'

He doesn't pause or turn.

'Bavar!'

He stops. Turns. Looks up. First time I can see anything beneath all the hair.

And wow.
Those eyes.
That face.
Like heartbreak, all pooled in one place.

Bavar

Run. Run. Staggering, stumbling run. She saw me. She saw past the other stuff. I saw her eyes widen, saw the brightness of her shock.

'Bavar!'

Her voice, so light and clear; her footsteps flying after mine. She's quick – I have to stretch my legs. What does she want with me? Nobody ever chased me before; nobody even *saw* me before. I run further than I need to, just to lose her, just so she won't follow me home. She's determined, but gradually I outpace her. And then I have to turn back and head home, my breath hot in my chest, my legs burning, looking out for her as I round every corner.

'Bavar!' my aunt exclaims as I walk up the drive towards the yellow house. 'You're late! But look at you – you've grown in a day!' Her voice thrills with it, and I shirk back, my cheeks flushing. Then she frowns. 'And where . . . where is the lunch basket, Bavar? Were you chased? Did you lose it?'

So of course then I have to show her where the basket is, and she wants to know why I hid it there.

Angel

I have to remind myself that I'm the new me now. Sometimes the old me is so close, it's like she's breathing down my neck, and I have to literally shrug her off my shoulders.

Man, does she cry.

She's trying now, even though the new me has strictly forbidden it.

I'm back at the house. It's a nice house. The people here are nice. They have grown-up children of their own and thought it would be good to do something positive for others not so fortunate.

I'm not so fortunate. You wouldn't have known that a year ago. I didn't know it a year ago. Anyway. The best thing is to think of other things. And the best thing right now is to think of Bavar. He's like a murder mystery in boy form. I want to know who done it: Who made his eyes ache like that? Who made him hide in his collar? I want to know where they are, and why they did it.

Sometimes people don't know they're doing that kind of thing. Killing someone on the inside. My parents would have been horrified if they knew they were going to do that to me. Of course they didn't mean to, but I'm not sure that helps. It makes it hard to be angry with them, and sometimes . . . sometimes I really need to be angry with them. They're the villains of my murder mystery. They killed me on the inside when they died like that. It was them.

The nice people are called Pete and Mary. They wear bright stripy jumpers, and jeans with no shape, and they like gardening, and cups of tea, and cake. Their grown-up children both live in America, and they're very proud and they miss them very much, and I wonder – if it's all so nice and happy, then why did they both go so far? If I'd grown up and they were still here, I'd never go. I'd never go all the way to America.

I shrug my shoulders, swallow more tears and think of Bavar again. Man, can he run. You can really see how tall he is when he runs like that. Taller than any grown man I've seen. About seven foot, I reckon. Or nearly, anyway.

I'm going to keep up with him tomorrow. I'm going to wear my trainers to school specially.

Bavar

I'm not going to go into it. All there is to say is that I'm taking the basket to school. I'm going to have to lose it in the bike rack or something. Aoife and I fell out about it, and it's the first time in a really long time that I'm angry about something. That I've felt anything about anything. It burns my cheeks and I notice I'm striding as I walk to school. So I slow down, and fold myself in a bit, and by the time I get there I'm feeling OK.

And then I realize, once I'm in the corridor, that I've still got the flipping basket. Nobody else notices, so that's fine. But the new girl lights up when she sees me with it.

'Ooh, what you got in there?' she asks. 'Strawberries and champagne? Some horses doofers?'

'Horses . . . ?'

'Hors d'oeuvres, they call them,' she says, a flicker of something crossing her face. She shrugs. 'Posh food.'

'No. Nothing like that.'

I turn my back on her and busy myself hanging the thing up, and manage to cover it with my coat and I'm just about feeling normal again and I turn around and she's still there.

'Don't look so afraid,' she says. 'I'm not after your lunch.'

I just look at her. And I try to work out what she's doing here. Why she's talking to me. Why I'm still standing here, even.

And then I walk away.

14

Angel

I do kind of like the way he refuses to say anything and then just walks off. It's a bit like saying, 'Whatever – I don't have the time for this,' without actually saying it.

I usually have to say these things out loud – for the satisfaction of it, if nothing else. Last night Nice Mary told me off for swearing. She called me a potty mouth! And I laughed, and she did not find it even remotely funny, so I had to spend some time in my room after dinner. Which was absolutely fine with me.

She tried to 'talk' to me after. About the thing that happened. I don't know who needed it; I didn't feel like it was me. So I didn't oblige her. I kept it all inside.

Truthfully, I don't know what I'd say. And I want to keep it all in anyway. It's mine. It's all I have left. So anyway, she sat next to me on the bed and I ignored her, concentrated instead on the flowers on the wallpaper, and remembered the way I could see Bavar's spine through his white shirt. The way it curved.

'Now, Angel, I know how hard this is for you,' she started, putting her hand on the pale pink duvet cover. I looked down, and the old me flinched inside, because how could this be happening? How was it that this was the person with me, her broad hand next to mine, her whole self warm and real and alive and just so easily *here*. I stared at her hand, willing it to change; for the fingers to be longer, more slender, the skin paler. To be wearing the slim gold ring I now wear on my forefinger. *That*. That was the hand I wanted next to mine, not this clumsy great *ham* of a hand. A heaviness gathered in my throat and at the back of my eyes, and I thought if I had to sit there with her a moment longer I might have to scream and stab her with the pen I'd been using.

'Do you?' I asked, looking her straight in the eye. 'Do you really know?'

And that shut her up.

I watch Bavar walk away from me now, into his form room. I know I'll see him next period, in English, and the thought makes me smile.

Bavar

English is a nightmare. She watches me the whole time and it makes my spine twitch. I try to concentrate on *Lord of the Flies*, but their madness is a pale thing compared to the heat of her eyes on my back. And after a while something inside me, something that's curled up and hidden for so long, begins to stretch.

So I leave.

I just get up, in the middle of class, grabbing my bag and charging past the teacher, out through the door, down the corridor. I thought I liked school before. It was quiet, and safe. Nobody challenging me; nothing about to end the world. It felt normal – and me being here, I guess that made me feel normal. Just for a little bit.

I have no idea how I'm feeling right now.

'Watch out!' snaps a boy as I collide with him. He looks older than me – year ten maybe. His tie is deliberately crooked; his hair arranged in little spikes.

'Sorry!' I say, and my voice comes out a bit louder than I meant it to.

He looks up, and then up a bit more, and then he turns pale, a confused expression on his face.

People don't normally really see me. It unsettles them. I can't possibly be this tall, this big. That can't be magic, spinning like dust in the air around me, because magic doesn't really exist.

Only it does.

The boy takes a step back and raises his hands as if I'm going to hurt him. I don't; I've never hurt anyone. I just stare at him until he runs away, nearly colliding with a bunch of kids coming the other way. They scatter, looking from him back to me. A couple of them frown as their minds fight with the sheer impossibility of me, and I sigh and shove my hands into my pockets, and concentrate on being small, unseen.

Normally, I don't have to concentrate so hard. It was something my parents taught me on those rare occasions when we'd go into the town. *Be quiet. Be small,* they'd say. *You're incredible, a force of nature, but they won't see that. They don't see you the way we do. They'll only see your differences. Use a little magic, feel it wind about you; it doesn't take much. They don't really want to see you anyway.*

They were so proud of their differences. The power that rang in them, that made the rest of the world seem so slow and grey. Maybe I felt like that once, when I was a kid, but I got older, and they got brighter as their magic grew, and the brighter they were, the colder they were. And I hated that.

I missed them long before they were gone.

I stride out to the main gate now, and their voices are still ringing in my ears, and my heart is beating too fast, too loud, so I can't hear anything else. And I keep my eyes down, so I don't know if anyone's watching as shadows stretch around me, but it doesn't matter because I'm not giving in to it. I promised myself. I swore it. Deep down in the cemetery, in the old part where nobody goes any more, deep in the tangle of ancient trees where even the crosses have been laid to rest. I went there when the world was sleeping beneath the pale of the full moon and I looked down at all the names graven into old stone and I promised myself I would not be the monster they had delivered to the world. I swore I would not follow in their footsteps.

And if the house calls to me to break that promise, and the cemetery haunts my dreams, and the sky itself is full of their lament, school was the place that was quiet. It was still, and easy, until yesterday. Now she's there, and she sees me. She stares at me and makes me run, bump into people.

So that's the end of that.

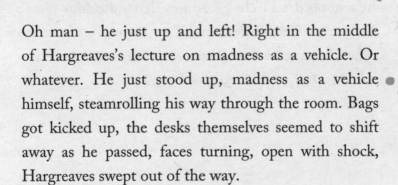

Angel

Oh man – he just up and left! Right in the middle of Hargreaves's lecture on madness as a vehicle. Or whatever. He just stood up, madness as a vehicle himself, steamrolling his way through the room. Bags got kicked up, the desks themselves seemed to shift away as he passed, faces turning, open with shock, Hargreaves swept out of the way.

Incredible.

To the extent that I just watched him leave without even thinking of following him.

'Well,' says Hargreaves, running his hand through his hair, his eyes a little wild. 'Back to the lesson please. I'm sure we'll see . . . uh. I'm sure he'll be back . . .'

He doesn't even remember his name.

Who *is* Bavar? I mean, how does this stuff just

happen? Why don't people register him properly, even when they've seen him?

And now the old me is having a proper battle with the new me. I want to leave. Follow in his footsteps and chase him. But the old me won't do it. She's stuck to the wooden chair, pen in hand, listening to Hargreaves drone on, knowing she isn't invisible, even if Bavar is. So there I sit. But a plan is forming. There's no way he's stopped mid-charge to get that ridiculous picnic basket. So I'll get it for him. I'll get his address from the office, because he was ill and went home and I need to take his stuff, and I'll go visit him.

Oh yes.

Bavar

I didn't mean to come straight home; it's way too early. I meant to wander for a bit, so Aoife wouldn't notice. But I was tired and I couldn't think of anywhere else I wanted to go, and suddenly the world seemed too small and I was sick of looking at pavements, so here I am.

'What happened?' she asks, as I walk into the hall.

This house is the right size for me. I see it with suddenly clarity. I've been pretending it isn't. That it's vast and cavernous and creepy, and that I'm not also those things too. After today, and that boy's face when we collided, I can see that I fit just fine here.

I look at Aoife for a long time, wondering what to say. How can I explain that everything is different, just because of one person? She stares back, her expression unchanging.

'There's a new girl,' I say eventually, feeling my cheeks get hot. And then I don't know what else to say. What does that even mean? How does that explain anything?

Aoife nods.

'A catalyst,' she says. 'And you didn't want it.'

I shake my head.

'Come,' she says. 'Come with me.'

I follow her into the kitchen and sit at the scarred pine table in the corner. There's a painting on the wall, an old oil of green fields beneath storm clouds, sheep clustered together beneath a wide-spreading tree. Hiding.

My storm is all around me.

'It's all right,' Aoife says, sitting opposite me. She's not bustling. Not making tea, cutting cake. She's just sitting, looking at me. Her dark hair is pulled back from her face, greying at the temples. She's not so different from my mother. From her daytime face, anyway.

'How?'

'It just is,' she says with a lift of her shoulders. 'You cannot control everything, Bavar. You are becoming what you were always meant to be. I've seen how hard you fight it . . .'

'I made a promise.'

She shakes her head.

'I made a *promise*.' My voice rises, and her eyes widen as she hears just a hint of the thing deep within.

'A promise? To whom?'

'To the world . . . To . . . I don't know. I made a promise, to myself, that I wouldn't fight; I wouldn't be like they were.'

'A promise cannot change what you are, Bavar.' She stares at me, and her eyes are bright, and I don't want to see what is reflected in them. She thinks I can be like them, and still be me, not be a monster. But she's wrong. She has never felt the way the power corrupts. She was the younger sister; the power didn't come to her.

I scramble up from the table, knocking it askew. Aoife clasps her hands together as I rise to my full height.

'One day,' she calls out, standing as I flee the room, her voice bright. 'One day you'll be glad of your true nature. You'll need it, Bavar!'

I roar as I head up the stairs. I can't help it. The

sound reverberates all around me, and the portraits of my ancestors up high on the walls tremble, and the painted faces stretch their mouths wide and roar with me.

It's a flipping disaster.

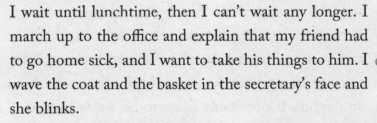

Angel

I wait until lunchtime, then I can't wait any longer. I march up to the office and explain that my friend had to go home sick, and I want to take his things to him. I wave the coat and the basket in the secretary's face and she blinks.

'Please?' I say. 'It's January – he'll need his coat tomorrow, when he's better.'

I mean to say – as if I care he wears a coat! Frankly, it's enormous and really heavy and I'd rather not take it. But it seemed a better excuse than the basket. What you going to say about a basket? He might need it for his baking?

'Bavar, you say,' she turns to the computer screen. 'Bavar. What's his surname?'

'Uh . . .'

'Oh, here he is. Bavar. That is his surname. And his . . .' She frowns. 'Must have missed something on the entry form . . . here we are, Meridown House, Dragon Hill.'

'Thank you!' I bustle out of the door before she can think again . . . about how if we were friends I'd know where he lives, or I'd have his number.

What sort of a house does a boy like that live in? I picture a great Gothic mansion, all spires and chimneys and leering gargoyles, and a gaunt old butler opening a creaking door. And it gives me a little thrill inside, even just the imagining of it. The reality's probably going to be a bit of a let-down, I tell myself, as I head up the hill. It's probably going to be a safe little semi with net curtains. My breath steams in the winter air, and the pavement glitters with frost, and I'm kind of laughing at myself now, because what the heck am I doing, trudging up this hill with all this stuff, to find a boy who wants to hide? It's not the best idea I've ever had, but I keep going anyway, and then I get to the top of the hill and look up and there it is, *Meridown House* spelled out in great curved iron letters over a vast gate and *wow*.

Just wow.

It's the yellow house. The one on the hill. The one that screams Gothic trapped beneath a layer of sunshine paint. And here I am at the gate, with the coat and the basket, and puffing a bit, because it's a steep hill. Clouds are gathering over the jagged skyline of a hundred chimneys, and a shiver runs down my back, so I take a deep breath and turn my back on it for a minute. The lines of the town spread out beneath me, from the church along the river to the farms in the distance, houses to either side in neat little rows, all of it directly overlooked by the house. It's an amazing view, with the low winter sun making all the shadows stretch.

I look back at the house. It's incredible. Like something from a film, and I'm right here. Only thing is I haven't quite tried to get in yet. I mean, there's this huge gate, and I don't know if I should just go in, or if I should ring the brass bell at the side. I'm not sure I want to ring the bell; it seems a bit like overkill. Like I might ring in the end of the world, or something. But I've now been here for about ten minutes and I'm starting to feel a bit stupid, and cold. And I have this old coat, not to mention the basket.

I look up through the gate and count the windows

again. Ten full-length ones along the bottom, divided by the porch. Ten windows above, each the size of a normal house. Or you know, about that. And then the gable windows in the roof. And the chimneys, and the towers. And a couple of gargoyles thrown in. Leering figures carved in stone, climbing up the towers, perching on the roof tiles.

Something moves in one of the upstairs windows. I shiver and move away to the bank of grass that you could imagine goats grazing on. After a couple of minutes arguing with myself, I spread out the coat and sit on it, and open the basket, take out the roll. Ham. Quite good ham, actually. Not your wafer stuff. I sit back, munching and watching all the little people and the little cars going about their business, from my quiet spot up high on the hill. And then I eat the apple, assuming it's not a fairy-tale one and about to send me to sleep for a hundred years. Not that I'd mind that. But anyway, it's good. It's peaceful. And in a minute I'll ring the bell.

I am not eating that cake. Looks like raw liver.

Bavar

I'm in the bed, with the curtains drawn around it. Feels like a boat out at sea, but at least I'm not drowning in the boat any more. It's about the right size for me, I can see that now.

'This house is your house,' Uncle Sal's soft voice, a year ago, just after my parents went. His glasses obscured his eyes. 'We are its caretakers for the moment, and you are its master.'

'I'm twelve.'

'The house doesn't care about that, Bavar.' The smell of the leather chairs in the study, the shaft of sunlight through the stained glass, bleeding on to the carpet. The heat, and the sick feeling in my stomach. They'd really gone. After everything that happened, they'd just turned their backs on it all, left me here with an aunt I barely knew, and this funny little man who smelt of old books. 'It was always your destiny to be its master. One day, you will come into your own.'

'And now?'

'Now things will be quiet, for a time.'

'Now that they're gone.'

I needed to say it out loud. It didn't feel real. But Uncle Sal didn't contradict me. So. It was real.

'Do you miss them, Bavar?'

'No.'

Uncle Sal sighed. 'It's been difficult, I know. But we will be all right, Bavar. You and me, and your Aunt Aoife. We'll get on; it'll work out.'

Was it a statement, or was he seeking reassurance? I didn't know then. I don't know now. All I knew was that there was an expectation, somewhere. When it was time – when I was ready – he would listen to me. He would do as I bid. So would Aoife. So would the house.

I am Bavar, master-in-waiting. And I think the time is coming, whether I'm ready or not.

'Bavar!'

Aoife twitches the dark curtains aside, her narrow face suddenly appearing between embroidered vines and birds. 'Your catalyst! My, but she's a live one!' she crows, flapping at me and rushing across the room, going from window to window.

I put my book down.

'My what?'

'Catalyst! The girl! Come, see! She was at the gate, but she went – I thought she'd gone, but she's just sitting on the hill. She has your basket, Bavar! She's come to see you!'

I join Aoife at the window, and there she is. Sitting out there, just outside the wall, sitting on my coat, eating my lunch.

How did this happen? What's she doing? My coat stretches like a blanket around her; she's very small. Her pale hair shines in the sunlight. She puts her hand into the basket, starts to eat the apple.

Who *does* that?

I turn from the window, fed up with the whole day and planning on getting back into the bed, and then Uncle Sal comes out of his study, a frown on his round face.

'Off you go, Bavar,' he says.

'Pardon?'

'Stop hiding in the house and go and get your coat back, and that ridiculous basket.'

'I'm not going out there!'

'You are,' he says, his eyes flashing behind his glasses. He's a small man, but in this instant there's a new steel in him, something I've never seen before. 'You absolutely are. I am not going to sit by and watch you hide from everything for one minute longer. Besides, your aunt is disturbing my work with all this fluttering about.'

Aoife stiffens by my side and mutters something about 'work', and Sal rolls his eyes, and they don't often argue, but when they do the whole house joins in, ancestors howling from the portraits, lights flickering, windows rattling. So I make for the stairs, watched by the pale faces of those who came before me. And heckled by a couple of the more cranky ones.

Angel

'What are you doing?'

I jump up, the hairs on my arms bristling. I don't know how the heck someone so big can creep up on a person so effectively. He looks proper grumpy too, all looming and scowling and hiding behind his hair.

'Came to bring your coat and your basket.'

'And eat my lunch . . .'

He noticed. I smile. Just on the inside.

'Didn't think you'd mind. Saved you the cake.'

He snorts, digging his hands into his pockets. He's in the shadow of the wall that surrounds the house; I can only see portions of his face and body.

There's a long silence. I think he'd call it awkward, but I'm quite enjoying it.

'You can go now, then,' he says. He steps forward

and I dart out of his way. He shakes his head as if he expected that, and picks up the coat. He takes a look behind him, up at the nearest window. A couple of the shadows within flicker, and when I look back at him he's got his fists clenched by his sides. He takes a step back, a deep breath, and then he runs at the basket, catching it with his foot and launching it down the hill. 'There.'

He doesn't look at me, doesn't see that I'm grinning and just about jumping up and down with how brilliant he is. He just marches back to the gate.

'Bavar . . .'

'Yup.'

Standing with his back to me, the gate in front of him.

'Isn't it lonely?'

It just comes out. I swear I didn't plan on asking something so big. I swallow and move back as he turns to me, lifting his head.

Man. I will never get used to this boy.

'I'm accustomed to it,' he says. His voice is deep, slow. I wonder how often he really uses it. Who he talks to.

'Well, I'm not.'

'You?'

His surprise makes me cross. I mean, just because I don't walk with a lurch and bury my head in my shoulders doesn't mean I'm not going through things too. Does he think he's the only one who ever felt like he didn't fit?

Here, in this house, in these shadows, he fits.

I don't fit anywhere.

I turn my back and start down the hill.

But I know this isn't the last time I'll be here.

Bavar

She looks like she has the sun with her. That sounds silly. She's bright, and that was all I saw. Then she said the thing about being lonely and there was another side to her. Something injured and reaching, searching.

I do not regret the thing with the basket.

She bounces down the hill and takes the sun with her, and I turn back to the house, shivering. I have no idea who painted it yellow. Was it supposed to be a disguise? Bad things can't happen here, because it's yellow?

Hah.

'Bavar! Your lesson!'

Sleety rain begins to fall as I head inside, and Sal is hovering impatiently on the stairs. 'He doesn't like it when you're late,' he says, fidgeting with his waistcoat.

'I know,' I say, trudging past him. I try to forget about the girl and realize I don't even know her name. That's a good thing – I can't give it away if I don't know it. And I don't want *him* to have it. There's power in a name, he always says.

The house gets darker as I get higher, and the winding staircase at the top is cluttered with boxes and piles of unravelling books. I pick my way through them and put my shoulder against the door, shoving it open.

My father's library is cold. It doesn't breathe without him, there's a stillness that makes my skin itch. I glance at the fireplace and it leaps into flame with a pop.

The bust of my grandfather is covered with a cloth. It was sculpted by someone famous, a long time ago, and my father told me always to keep my eye on it.

I didn't know what that meant, back then.

I take a breath and pull the cloth away. It's an old tablecloth of Aoife's, with sunflowers on it. Grandfather would be mortified if he knew. He hates to be covered, but he hates most things, and this was necessary. He shouts a lot, if he's left free.

'BAVAR!' he booms now, as I back away from him. 'Just in time. I want to talk to you about the barrier. I'm not convinced you've been working hard enough . . .'

I sigh. He's obsessed with the barrier. It's important, I know that, but he must've said the same thing a million times in the last year.

'. . . It is your JOB, Bavar, to keep that barrier intact,' he continues. 'It was forged with this family's magic, once our magic had done the damage and opened the rift between worlds. It is the only thing that protects the lands around us from the foul beasts, and only YOUR magic will keep it strong and keep them restrained to the grounds here . . . Bavar! Are you listening? You must put your heart and SOUL into it!'

'I already do,' I sigh. The barrier is like a web around the estate, strands of magic that cover acres of land and stop the raksasa from getting through to the world outside. It took me a while, in the beginning, to get a feel for it. Now it's second nature, like feeling in the dark for a familiar light switch. Feeding magic into it, until it gleams in my mind, stronger than steel. 'It's fine . . .'

But he isn't listening; he's still lecturing. I sit on one of the leather chairs around the table and watch his mouth move. It's mesmerizing, the way the metal contorts, like watching a bronze river flow. Suddenly he breaks off, his nostrils widening.

'Humanity!' he roars. 'What is that? What is the difference, Bavar? What have you done?'

'Nothing,' I tell him, leaning back in the chair. Reminding myself he's just a chunk of metal. His eyes flash.

'You must tell me!' he shouts. 'Report, Bavar. Has there been humanity on the grounds? Did you bring one *home* with you? That ridiculous school. What a notion. The master of this house, going to a common human school! I don't know what AOIFE was thinking . . .'

He launches into another tirade. He doesn't like me going to school. He thinks I should spend my time cooped up here with him, growing stronger in magic, keeping the barrier strong, and learning how to fight the raksasa. He doesn't know about the promise I made, that I would never fight like my parents did. They failed to look after the barrier, and people died because of it. So I know it's important to get that right. But fighting is another thing entirely.

'There was a new girl,' I break in eventually, when he looks like he's about to explode with frustration. 'I didn't bring her home; she followed me, brought my coat. Aoife says she's a catalyst.'

She's blonde, and small, and she smells of hope. Possibility.

I don't tell him that bit.

'A GIRL, on the premises? A *human girl*?' He jiggles on the pedestal, his brow furrowing. He was a big man, my grandfather. He leans forward slightly in his pose, shoulders broad and powerful, face heavily lined, determined. Predatory.

'She was on the grass outside the wall. She didn't come in.'

'So. So. But the smell of her . . . it is here. She touched your coat; they will scent it, Bavar.' His voice drops to concern. 'Are you ready?'

'Ready?'

'The rift grows, I have warned you of that, and now you bring this human girl's SMELL into the house to further tempt them here. They will come through the rift in their dozens and they will strike at the barrier harder than ever – Bavar, are you ready to fight?'

'Yes,' I say. I look at the fire, so that I don't have to face him when I lie, but it catches my confusion and roars, flames shooting up the chimney, sparks flying out in all directions.

'You need better control of it all,' he grumbles, as I

42

tread on a couple of burning embers. 'The house picks up on your mood; you should know that by now. And you can't fight the raksasa with fire. They're part made of it. So you'll need to show your game face. Show me, Bavar!'

I stick my tongue out at him. His mouth twitches.

He's not completely humourless, my grandfather. He just tries to hide it.

'. . . and I've no idea what business Aoife has, bringing up notions of catalysts. Why would some insignificant VILLAGE girl be a catalyst?' he blusters, almost as if speaking to himself. 'How could she possibly be connected to us here at all?'

'Connected?'

'Can't have a catalyst unless there's a connection, can you, boy? What's she got to do with it all, eh?'

I stare at him, tired and confused for about the billionth time today, and he stares back, unblinking. And then the window blows open with a bang.

Hot, fetid air pushes in through the room. Huge wings beat over the house, darkness obscuring the stars. Raksasa. However much I shore up the barrier, it won't stop them getting through the rift.

'Get out there! Make it go!'

'It *will* go,' I say, sitting on the edge of the desk and curling my fingers around the polished wood. I don't look at him. I focus on the striped rug by the hearth. Orange, brown, yellow, blue. Orange, brown, yellow, blue . . .

'Bavar!'

'It can't do anything,' I say, keeping my voice level. 'The barrier is solid; I've been working on it, like you said. It can't go anywhere. If I go out there now, I'll only antagonize it, make it worse.'

'You cannot just hide away in here!' Grandfather flexes his chest, making the pillar wobble. 'Bavar, I command you!'

I swallow hard. 'It's my decision.'

The beating wings are like a heartbeat, a fluttering, broken heartbeat that speaks only of bad things coming. I wait until they quieten. Until the creature heads back to its home beyond the rift.

'You see?' I raise my head. 'We just have to wait them out.'

He snorts. 'You must show them your strength. Show them that there is a master here, who will fight with all of his might, as I did once. You may not stop them all that way, but you can make them FEAR you, and fewer will try. You cannot think just to hide in here forever.

'Not forever. Just for now.'

He isn't content, and we both know he's right – the day is coming when I'll have to face them, whether I want to or not.

Angel

I think I might have to move in with Bavar. No. I don't mean that, obviously. But maybe I could put up a tent on that patch of grass, just be there in the peace overlooking the town. Things feel OK there. Unchangeable.

Everything here is change, and I never liked change. Mary's macaroni cheese is made with all the best intentions, and orange cheese, and it's so wrong – it sticks in my mouth and makes my nose tingle.

'*Come on. It can't be that bad,*' says Mum's voice, amused. '*She probably thought it would be comforting.*'

But it isn't, I shout in my head. It's all wrong, it doesn't have bacon in it, and it's not stuck in mounds that you need a knife to cut.

I never said it was all perfect. Dad was away a lot,

with his research, and Mum was pretty busy herself, most of the time. And she wasn't much of a cook. But that was OK. It was normal. This is just wrong. The sounds are wrong too. Not so much of the chatter, more of the fork-scraping-plate sort. The floral curtains have been drawn and the carpet is vanilla and I feel like I've been imprisoned in a cake and I can't breathe.

I can't breathe here.

They're too quiet.

Pete clears his throat.

'So. How was your day, Angel?'

'OK.'

I stick a row of peas on to the fork tines; the pop of green skin is satisfying.

'Do you like the school? Our two were always . . .' He frowns. 'Well, they seemed happy enough there. Didn't they, Mary?'

'Have to go,' I mumble, lurching up from the table. 'Homework.'

'I'll bring a cup of tea in a bit,' says Mary behind me.

I imagine turning and letting out the scream that's on my chest, shocking her out of her tea-making comfort. But I don't. I head to my room, and I think about how Bavar suits his house, and how I don't suit this one. And then I pull the battered old suitcase out from under the bed, and the smell when I open it is of home and . . .

help

I take the posters out, and the ball of Blu-Tack, and I wage a war on all the pastel pretty of this room, and it takes me a while and some of the time I can't really see straight because of my traitorous crying eyes but I do it and I keep doing it and then it's done. I shove the candle in the skull on to the desk, and when Mary brings the tea, her mouth tightens a bit, but she doesn't say anything, and in a minute she brings matches, and a box of tissues, and she sits with me on the bed, looking up at it all, not touching me, just sitting there.

The new school is smaller than my old one. Smaller, and older. I kind of like it, the way the corridors tangle so you never quite know where you're going. Plenty of places to skulk. I wait for Bavar by his locker in the morning. Every so often, as the second hand ticks on the clock in the corridor, I tell myself I'm being stupid, like some crazy stalker fangirl, but I wait anyway, and when he arrives with a crash of the double doors, I have to stop myself smiling at the sight of him. I don't know why. Except I did think about it a bit last night and I reckon probably it's because seeing him is like proof that I'm not round the bend.

I didn't imagine it all last year. It wasn't burglars.

I just need to work out how it's all connected.

'No basket today?' I ask.

He gives me a blank look, as if he's never heard of a basket before, and then the bell rings and kids start to swarm around us. Well. They start to swarm around me; he's got some kind of invisible barrier around him, so they just avoid the space where he's standing entirely. After a second, fed up with stares and jostles, I move into his space.

'What are you doing?' he protests, as I shove right up against him.

'Hiding,' I say.

I suppose it's not the most dignified way to walk into a classroom, stuck tight against the side of the strangest boy in school, but it kind of works. Nobody looks up as we enter, nobody notices as we sit down. I mean, I don't sit in his lap, or anything, just pull a desk up close to his and sit as close as I can.

And then I see it, right there, though he's ducked

his head down and his hair is hiding most of his face. He's smiling.

'Why don't they see you?' I whisper at him.

'They don't want to,' he says.

I pull out my folder, plant it on the desk in front of my face.

'But *why*?'

He gives me a long look. His dark eyes glitter.

'Why do you think?'

'Because you're different?'

He nods.

'But lots of people are different. So it must be more. Is it magic?' I grin, as if I'm joking. 'Or are you some kind of monster?'

The grin falls, my chest burns, and I guess we both wish I hadn't asked that question. Because he isn't saying no, and I *knew* that monsters existed. I just didn't expect to be sitting next to someone who smelt like them, in my normal school day.

It brings it all back.

Makes it real.

They all said it couldn't be real. They said it was all in my head.

I look at Bavar. He's not in my head.

'You're not, are you?' I whisper.

'No,' he says. 'No, I'm not.'

Of course I lose him at lunchtime. I turn around to put my stuff in my bag, and when I look up he's gone. And everybody's staring, because I'm new and I don't fit and man, I used to fit. Before that night.

I don't care.

I don't care.

I hold my head high as I stalk past them all, and then I take my lunch and sit under the staircase on the science corridor and I make myself eat it, looking at all the different kinds of shoes people wear to school, the way they all walk, and after a while I can breathe again and then there's a shadow over me and when I look up Bavar is there, stooping down, head tilted.

'Why are you eating your lunch here?'

I shrug.

'Are you *hiding*?'

'Maybe . . .'

'Why do you need to hide?'

I sigh, staring at him. 'Why do you think you're the only one who wants to?'

He's silent for a while and I think maybe he'll leave,

but he doesn't. He just lingers there, making us both uncomfortable.

'Just come and sit, or something; you're making me nervous,' I say in the end.

'I thought it might help, if I was here,' he grunts, trying to fold himself into a very small space beside me. 'Stop people seeing you, or something.' He stares at me, blows his cheeks out. 'I don't know.'

'Did you never speak to a person before?'

'Not here,' he says. 'I mean, not . . . not a person like you . . .'

'You're a bit hopeless at it.'

'And yet here we are,' he says, the hint of a smile on his face. 'Speaking.'

'Hey, new girl,' comes a new voice. A girl, tilting her head to look into our hiding place. 'Why you hiding in there?'

She ignores Bavar as he scrambles out, shifting to one side to let him pass, her eyes still fixed on me. She doesn't seem to register him at all.

She definitely sees me though.

'I was just having my lunch . . .' I start.

'There's a cafeteria, you know,' she says, her voice full of scorn. 'With tables and chairs, and *everything*.'

I grab my stuff and scuttle out of my hiding place, standing to face her. Her eyes glint with malice and I fold my arms, wondering what she's going to do next.

'I was going to ask you,' she says, looking me up and down. 'What kind of name is *Angel*?'

It doesn't sound as if she really likes the name Angel. It's become something twisted and ridiculous, the way she says it.

'What do you mean?' I ask, trying to keep my voice nice and light, despite the thump of my heart in my ears. I was kind of expecting trouble at some point, after my little lie-fest on day one. It's taken a couple of days to build, and now here she is. Grace something, I think, ready to take me on. She has brown hair down to her waist, shiny and immaculate. She swishes it back over her shoulders in a practised move.

The funny thing is that I told *her* the truth. I lied to lots of people on that first day, but when she started up with the same old questions I got fed up of it all, so I told her exactly what happened, and that I was now living with foster parents. And I had a smile on my face at the time – I guess I was nervous – so *she* was the one who called me out as a liar. Which is ironic, really.

'What kind of parents call their kid Angel?' she asks now.

'The kind that later orphan her,' I say.

'That kind of thing's not funny,' she whispers, leaning in to me. 'You shouldn't joke about it.'

'I'm not joking,' I tell her.

She advances on me, and then there's a little blur to my left, and the world spins.

I'm outside, in front of the bike racks, and Bavar is standing before me, slightly out of breath. The school field behind him is misted with frost, and shadows stretch from the trees towards us. For a second it's like the world is black and white, all angles and lurking things, and he's the thing that stands between all of that and me.

The only thing.

I blink, and my head clears, the world starts to move again, kids jumbling past us, their heads down, laughing and battering at each other with bags and coats.

'What was that?' I whisper.

'You looked sad.'

'I was angry!'

'Sad,' he says, shaking his head obstinately.

'So you've just propelled me out here? How did you do that? And what am I supposed to do now? Walk back in and pretend nothing happened?'

He shrugs. '*She* probably will. She'll just think you ran off, or something.'

I stare at him.

'People don't like it,' he says. 'They pretend it isn't happening. *Most* people, anyway – what's different about you? Are you really called Angel?'

'Yes, I really am,' I say. 'And I could ask you the same question – what's different about *you*?'

He stands there looking at me, the shadows stretching around him. He seems to grow in that moment, and I tell myself he doesn't frighten me, but all the little hairs on my arms are standing up because whatever that was, and however he did it, he *did it*. And it smelt of the monsters who came that night; it smelt of magic – dark and intoxicating.

'Bavar . . .'

But I don't know what to say. I don't know where to start. And while I'm struggling to find the words, he turns and walks away.

Bavar

I saw her in danger.

An angel, in danger.

It was all I saw, and the thing I've been denying all my life reared up. The world got darker, and she was the only bright thing. She was in danger, so I took her and I got her out of there. It was a rush of energy, a rush of blood to the head, something, I don't know. I never did anything like that before.

And now she's angry, and I'm confused. I always knew I didn't fit in this world, but I thought I was the only one. That only someone like me wouldn't fit. She doesn't fit either. She's all the right things on the outside, but something on the inside is different, like it's seen things that it shouldn't have seen, and so now she doesn't fit.

What did she see, that made her like that?

I can't stop replaying it in my head. That look on her face. The twist in my gut, and that thing inside – the thing that knows how to fight and how to kill . . . that thing is no longer content to curl up silent and small. It doesn't care about the promise I made.

It's ready for a fight.

Angel

I take my time walking back to the nice house after school. My head's still spinning. I breathe slow, and the world is quiet around me, winter-slow, the sky bleak, trees unmoving. A normal November day, in a normal town. Except it isn't. The yellow house perches above it all, and as I turn to look up at it, dozens of large black birds take flight from the frozen ground next to me, wheeling up into the sky like shards of night, swooping low over the rooftops.

Is that normal? I feel like it's hard to tell now. Before, I would have told myself it was just a strange bird thing, but now it feels like it means something. It means monsters, and magic. Or maybe I'm going crazy – it's hard to know. It's like I've learned to hide from myself. I can be alive on the outside, and doing all the normal stuff, and on the inside . . . well, it's a bit of a wasteland, really. Think of blackened trees and yellow, dusty earth. That's what happens when you shut down. When bad stuff happens, and you have no control over it. And you hid in the cupboard, because your dad told you to, and you were a good girl so you did what you were told, but now you wish, *wish*, you hadn't been so good, because hiding in the cupboard meant that they died.

And you didn't.

I remember the sound of great flapping wings. Like a giant moth, battering at the bedroom window until it smashed, and there was glass all over the floor. I sat up and Mum and Dad rushed in, and there was a screech like a thousand nails being dragged over a board that made my spine turn to ice. A stench of metal, and darker things, and a warp in the air that made it hard to see. And Dad hustled me into the cupboard and I was too numb to argue, too dumb to do anything else.

I put my hands over my ears, when Mum screamed. And I didn't hear anything else, and I didn't even open my eyes until someone grabbed me, and I started screaming then, fighting and biting, but the voice was calming, and I realized after a while that it was a woman in uniform, a police woman, and she pulled me out of there, and she held me tight to her side, and she wouldn't let me look. We walked over broken glass and around spools of darkness shining wet in the moonlight. Her black boots, my bare feet.

I never saw them.

They said it was a violent burglary, a burglary gone wrong. But I knew. I knew it was something unnatural.

I wish I'd stayed with them. I wish I'd fought with them. And I'm not delusional. I know I wouldn't have made any difference – no human could have fought that creature. But I would have tried. And whatever happened, I could have held on to that.

'Angel!'

I start. Mary is waiting for me at the door. All my senses fire up at the look of worry on her face.

'What? What happened?'

'Nothing,' she says. 'You looked like you were sleepwalking. I wondered if you were going to walk right into the pond!'

I look down at the pond in front of my feet. It's about the size of a pound coin. Well. Maybe a bit bigger, but still. I probably would have survived it.

'Come on, come in,' she says. 'I got crumpets . . . do you like them?'

I look at her; my heart is in my throat. I like crumpets. Who doesn't like crumpets?

But what if she does them wrong?

'Can I do them?' I ask.

She grins. She has a kind face. Brown eyes, round cheeks, curly hair.

'Yes!'

Up in my room, crumpet disaster neatly averted by yours truly, who knows how to wield a butter knife. Dinner was OK too. Pete was out, and somehow it was easier, just Mary and me, the TV on in the background. It was OK. I even saw the cat, Mika, for a moment or two before he showed me his bottom and left for better things. I didn't blame him.

I took his lead and told Mary I needed to do homework, and she made me help with the dishes, which was criminally boring, but after that I managed to escape to my room, and I've lit the candle in the skull and got my maths book out and I'd sort of planned on ignoring everything that happened today, but I can't stop thinking about Bavar, and that warp in the air when he got me away from Grace today.

'Something's going on,' I murmur.

Something . . . Dad's voice, all intrigued, like when he was in the middle of researching a new legend and all passionate about it, flinging his arms out with descriptions of things I thought only lived in his imagination.

Bavar must be connected, somehow, with what happened that night to my parents.

I spent so much time being told it was all in my head. After it happened, when every night was a nightmare and every day was just the grey in-between. Dad always talked about what we didn't know; all the things we told ourselves weren't really out there, because we were too afraid to see the truth. Mum and I would listen and nod, and wink at each other, because it lit a fire in his eyes and we loved him for it, but we knew it was all just a myth, really. Like chasing ghost stories.

And then it happened, and they were gone, and I couldn't just laugh it off. I felt so bad for not believing him, and I didn't want the rest of the world to do that any more, I had to wake everybody up. I was full of it, couldn't stop talking about it. What I'd seen, what they were all too stupid to realize. Of course nobody believed me, they thought it was grief making me sick. Even when I'd given up on them and stopped talking, still it wouldn't leave me alone. Not in my dreams.

I've tried being normal, I really have. But it's awful, because sometimes, when I miss them with an ache that might swallow me up, when my throat is howling with no sound because it's so tight with all the want of it, sometimes there is *nothing* that makes sense. Nothing for tomorrow, or the day after, or the day after that. It's just silent. And nothing gets through that – not school, not Mary, or Pete. Not the other kids, or the teachers, they've got no chance.

But now there's Bavar, and he just shouts questions in my face with all his own silence and his hiding. And so I don't care about normal any more. I care about *this*. I need to know, what it is with him and the monsters. I need to know more than I need anything else right now.

I sit on my hands. I should sit here and do my homework, steer well clear of Bavar, and whatever is going on. I've seen enough. Been through enough. Mary and Pete won't like it if I go out wandering in the dark alone. Bavar won't like it. And I'm not even sure what it is I want to find. I mean, monsters, and boys who can move like lightning? It's films and books and TV shows, not actual feet-on-the-ground truth. Right?

I stare at the skull. Its eyes flicker.

'Right?'

WRONG.

I close the maths book with a sigh. I'm going to have to do it, even if it's not the right thing. I need to.

I wait until I hear Pete get in, and then I call down to say goodnight, and I put some things in my rucksack: gloves, a cereal bar, some water. The catapult I made with Dad, when I was about seven. And then I sit on the bed, breathing through my fingers, and listen to the sounds of them using the bathroom, going to bed. It's awful. They don't do things the right way. The sounds aren't quite as they should be; they're too quiet, too measured. There are no heated discussions between them, no bickering about who should go back down because the kitchen light is still on. Just the muted sounds of people getting into bed, picking up a book.

I sit for longer, longer, longer than I think I possibly can, and then, when even the muted sounds are gone and all I can hear is the creak of radiators cooling, I creep down the stairs and out into the street.

Bavar

It's getting harder to ignore them, when they come through the rift and strike at the barrier, trying to get through to the world outside. The thing inside me wants to fight them. I have to remind myself that I want to hide, and keep the barrier intact. That's all. The idea is that if I stay hidden, they won't have anything to get hold of. No fear, no humanity, no smell of blood to tempt them further. They'll come, and the barrier around the estate will hold, and they'll go back again, thwarted.

Aoife wants me to fight. To show them what they should be afraid of, to send them fleeing with no doubt about who is in charge. She thinks I can be a master as Grandfather was, strong and wise. She never saw the way my parents fought them, beast against beast, tooth and claw, to the death. They were terrifying.

I never wanted to fight.

'Fighting is in the spirit,' Grandfather says, looming at me as I sit on the library floor, poring over his old diaries – what he calls *Wisdom on the Art of the Master*. Nothing ever got past him, in his day. He kept the barrier intact, fought every monster down, and somehow never let it change him. It all went wrong when he died. He says it was his fault, he didn't teach Mum properly, and that's why she neglected the barrier. She let the magic build inside her instead, used it just for the fight and the glory, and it corrupted her. So now he's determined to get it right with me. 'Your body was made to fight, Bavar, but it cannot do it alone. You need to put your *spirit* into it.'

'I'm doing OK.'

'Worlds were not saved by boys doing OK. Battles cannot be won without a little passion, a little pride, Bavar! You are the master of this house, connected to all of its magic! You cannot keep on hiding away like this, and now they have scented this *girl* they will be more bloodthirsty than ever. You must fight to turn them back, before they come in force!'

If he had hands, they would be gesticulating wildly.

As it is he has to content himself with rocking on his pedestal for emphasis.

'Do you wish they'd made more of you?' I ask.

'WHAT?'

I wonder if his ears are malformed. I've wondered it before – sometimes he shouts at random and it makes me jump. Actually, maybe that's why he does it.

'Arms. Legs. You could have done more,' I say.

'Arms and legs!' he splutters. 'It is not my job to have arms and legs! Not my job to do more, Bavar – it is yours! You have arms and legs, and what do you use them for? Writing, and walking to that *school* of yours.'

'School's OK.'

'Why?' He narrows his eyes.

I shrug. 'I like geography.'

'GEOGRAPHY! I'll tell you about geography! If you want geography, there are atlases, globes.' A large amber globe on the reading table starts to whirl, the silver lines of continents gleaming as it goes. 'There are books,' he barks, as they start to leap from the shelves, 'all about the world. You do not need school for that!'

'They're all about two hundred years old!' I shout, ducking as they thud to the floor all around me, pages speckled brown with age.

'What's wrong with that?' he simmers.

'I'm living now. In the now, Grandfather.'

'Well, and so you are. With Aoife and that little husband of hers. And this school, that they have insisted upon.' He blows out his bronze cheeks. 'Which is apparently now teaching you to be rather impertinent. Let us turn to the real things. This world that you're living in – this *now* of yours – is all very well, but it won't count for TOFFEE if you cannot protect it from the raksasa that crave its possession!'

'What if I don't want to?'

'This is your job; this is what you are,' he says, sighing at the familiar words. 'The world is relying on you. Your PARENTS are relying on you . . .'

'My parents!' I burst. Like it means anything, like I owe them anything. I take a breath, as he stares at me. 'We don't even know they're alive.'

'We'd know,' he says firmly. 'We'd know if they were dead. They're out there somewhere, fighting.'

It was all about the fight for them. The fight, and the parties afterwards. They enjoyed it too much, and others paid the price when the raksasa broke free. The death of innocents on their hands, they weren't prepared for that. They were too slow – by the time they caught up with the escaped monster, the damage was already done. No magic could undo it. So they slayed the creature, flung their magic into the barrier, and then they left to fight on the other side of the world.

'It's no good,' my mother said that day in a low whisper, her eyes on the ground, holding my father's hand, knuckles white, ancient, misshapen bags at their feet, the engine of the car rumbling outside. The bright sun shining through the door, and the portraits all deathly silent, watching us fall apart. 'We cannot change now, Bavar. We are fit for the fight, and nothing else.' My father just stood there by her side, no words, only dark, glittering eyes full of torment. 'Aoife was always wiser than me, she will care for you better, and we will find our fight somewhere else, somewhere remote, where humanity is not so close.'

I watched them leave. Watched the car wind through the streets of the town, getting smaller and smaller. Watched my whole life just drive away.

'You don't know they're fighting,' I say to Grandfather now, pushing it all away with an effort. 'You don't have any idea what they're up to, do you?' I look at him as I ask it, and for a second imagine that he does know, and he's about to tell me that it's all

OK, and they're different now, softer, like they were sometimes when I was small.

'Does it make it better, to constantly scratch at it?' he sighs, his bronze eyes shining. 'You cannot change it, and neither can I. Here we are, you and I. Now, can we proceed? How will you fight the raksasa, Bavar? Show me!'

I stand, and the shadows swing as my head hits the chandelier. There's that feeling inside, where the magic lies, where the fighter in me lives. I reach in and pull on that feeling, and that's when the Bavar they all want comes out. I show him a few moves, feel the stretch in my limbs, and then I close my eyes and imagine I really was facing one of the raksasa, with its burning eyes and blood-red skin, its enormous batwings battering at the sky above, and suddenly Angel is there, and it all gets a bit confused in my head.

There's a clatter, a muffled curse, and then a great crash.

'*There's* a bit of spirit!' says Grandfather, face down on the hearth rug. 'Bit of work needed at direction, unless –' he grimaces as I pick him up – 'unless that's what you were intending?'

'Uh, no,' I say, putting him back on the pedestal. 'Sorry.'

'Good job I'm not made of CLAY,' he rumbles. But he's pleased. I can tell from the extra wrinkles around his eyes. He is pleased, and I am one step closer to being just what he wants me to be.

Even when I was small, I never really wanted any of this. My parents would talk to me about it, and their eyes would gleam, and their smiles would get sharp with a kind of hunger I never understood, and I think they thought it would be exciting. A fairy tale, and I was the hero. But it never felt like that. It felt like nightmares knocking at the windows. It felt like they weren't my parents, when they fought. They were something else entirely, and I didn't like it. I didn't like the way they shone with it, so I swore to myself I would never fight like that. I would find another way. But the thing inside is awake now, and it wants to reach out and send them fleeing, terrified, back to their own world. So tonight when the raksasa breaks free of the rift and screeches in the sky above the house, I head out on to the roof, just to see. Just to know for myself what it feels like to face one.

Angel

Wow, it's cold. And I'm not afraid, but it's creepy being out at night. It's such a quiet town, seems like everyone's in bed already. The streets are empty, dark but for the rounds of orange beneath the lamps, everything rimed in frost.

I look up at the moon, trapped behind shifting clouds.

It's lonely.

I did have friends, before. I mean, not that many; I wasn't exactly Miss Popular. But I had a couple. Liv was the one who tried the hardest afterwards. We used to spend evenings together when her mum was working, she'd come over and we'd do stuff, listen to music, paint our nails. Watch scary TV, when Mum was distracted with marking. She called a few times, when I was in the other place. But I wasn't me then. I was deep down inside myself, hiding.

Couldn't go back to that school. Skived a bit, refused to go to lessons.

So they moved me here, to the nearest town. New start.

Now here I am, chasing boys who smell of monsters.

'That's about right,' I say out loud.

I wonder what Mum and Dad would make of it. I mean, they wouldn't be big fans of me being out at night on my own, obviously, but I wonder what they'd think of Bavar. Dad would be all over him with curiosity, and Mum would like him, I think. She likes everyone. Even the ones a bit hard to like, she likes them especially.

Liked.

My nose starts to prickle.

But no. This is my adventure. This is me, getting the truth, and then it will all make sense, somehow. It will all be OK. That's what they say, isn't it, when they run out of words. 'It will be OK.'

A shriek tears the world apart, and I stagger to the nearest lamp post and hang on, and for a second I'm caught, I'm stuck in that cupboard again, but I force myself to move. I stretch my legs like they're spaghetti, I plough through the air, pushing against gravity, running up the road, running up the hill, and there's the house, and every window blazing, and the sky above is boiling amber clouds and up on the roof the shape of a boy, and the enormous dark, winged shape of something from my nightmares.

And they're fighting.

They're *fighting*.

And I can't breathe. I can't do *anything*. I try to push myself forward – I want to climb the gate and climb the house, and get up there and FIGHT with him but my body isn't listening, and then I realize the boy on the roof *isn't* fighting, he's just crouching there, defending himself as the monster attacks with claws and wings and that shriek that should wake the whole town. Over and over the creature darts at the huddled shape, its great jaws wide, serrated teeth catching that strange orange light, steam rolling off its sinewy bat-like body. Over and over, darting, and wheeling away again, its blood-red wings great booming sails that catch at the boy's cloak, so that he is constantly shifting just to stay alive.

But he doesn't fight.

Why doesn't he fight?

'Bavar!'

My voice is small, it's a tiny embarrassing husk, there's no way it can be heard above the flap of those monstrous wings, and the shriek of the monster-call.

But the boy-shape turns towards me, and thrusts out an arm as he does, and the monster is knocked away. It spins, howling, and heads for the burning sky, and Bavar watches it go, his fists clenched by his sides, and then he turns back to me and roars, lion-deep and angry as hell.

And, dagnamit, I run back down the hill and back to the nice house, my breath tearing in my chest, and I was right there, I even had the catapult, and everything, and I just ran away.

I can barely look at myself in the mirror, when dawn finally takes over the skies and it's time to face another day. I swore I'd fight, the first chance I got, and I didn't.

And neither did Bavar.

I open the bedroom door, mainly to get away from myself, and Mika's there, black coat gleaming in the early morning sun.

'Hi,' I whisper, crouching down. 'How are you?'

He butts his face up against my knee and starts to purr.

'Life treating you well then,' I say, running my hand over his back. He drops to the floor and shows me his belly, rubbing his head against the carpet. Black hair, vanilla carpet. 'Naughty,' I smile, reaching out and stroking him. He purrs. If only people were so simple. I mean, you'd think Bavar would *want* a friend. Stuck away in that massive house, hiding from monsters.

Why does he hide, anyway? He looks like he could hold his own, even against those things. I shudder, remembering the almost-human shape of the creature's body, its enormous wings and that sulphurous smell that took me right back to that night. I'm not going to hide away though, not again. I'm going to get to the bottom of it all. I'm going to find out how Bavar is connected with what happened to my parents, and I'm going to fight. The catapult is a child's toy, but I don't care. I'll fight with everything I have, if I get another chance. After I've got through the school day, that is.

'Hey, Angel!'

I start, and turn to see Grace coming towards me, long hair swinging, bag flapping against her side.

'Hi,' she says.

'Hi.' I keep on walking, and she falls in next to me.

'I'm sorry about the other day,' she says. 'I didn't realize.'

'Realize what?'

'About your parents, that it was true. Mum said you were living with the Frazers because . . . well. You know.'

I carry on walking. It's cold, and I didn't bring that much winter stuff with me. Mary made me borrow a scarf, and it's itchy, and it smells of her, which I'm not quite sure I'm one hundred per cent enjoying.

'So what happened to them?' Grace asks.

I stop, turn to her. 'What?'

'Your parents. I just wondered,' she says quickly, catching the look on my face. 'That's all.'

'Burglary,' I say, turning and marching on towards school. The pavements sparkle with frost, and my boots crunch against them. Big black boots, to keep my feet on the ground. Mum always laughed at my boots. She said they made my legs look like golf clubs.

'And you were there? Mum said . . .'

'Your mum says a lot.'

'Yeah.'

I look sideways at her. I can't tell whether she's trying to be friendly or collecting gossip.

'So were you, there?'

'Yes.'

'Oh. That must have been . . .' She looks up as we reach the school gates. A tall blonde girl is waiting and looks at us with a puzzled expression, raising an eyebrow at her. 'Well,' says Grace. 'I just thought I'd say hi. See you in there.' She runs off to join the other girl, and I follow them at a distance, my eyes out for Bavar. I had this whole speech ready, about not roaring at friends, and how we can fight those creatures together. But he doesn't come in to school at all, and that's far worse than anything Grace could ever say or do.

Bavar

I've never skipped a day of school before, not since Sal suggested I start there last year. Aoife was a bit sceptical, and Grandfather was horrified, but they always avoid Grandfather anyway, so they just ignored his shouting, and I covered him with the tablecloth to keep him quiet. Aoife went ahead and enrolled me, and after a while it didn't seem so strange. After a while it seemed like about the only thing that really made sense. It was a good place to be, away from the monsters and the madness of this house.

Now it's different. Angel saw me, and now she's seen the raksasa too. She stood there and shouted my name, and the creature smelt her blood, and I panicked and hit out, to stop it hurling itself at the barrier, to stop it getting to her. My fist against its warm skin, and magic leapt between us, and it wheeled away instantly. I won. But now there will be more. Now they have smelt human blood, now they have felt my power, sensed my fear.

Aoife made what she calls my favourite supper when I got in last night, because she was proud of me. She doesn't understand why I don't want to fight.

'It's what generations of our family have done,' she said, flitting around the kitchen as I sat at the table and thought of those amber eyes, the red of its skin, the sail-like wings that make a sound I can't describe. 'They have fought, to protect this town – to protect the world! Your parents would be proud, Bavar. And I mean that in a good way. They weren't all bad.' She set a platter before me, its ivy pattern completely obliterated by the huge, bloody steak she had barely cooked, a sprig of green on top. My stomach rolled.

'I know you have doubts,' she said, pouring boiling water into a huge brown teapot as Uncle Sal came in. 'But you can do this, Bavar. You can do whatever you set your mind to, and you can do it all in your own way. That's what going to school is all about. Remember? So that you would know humanity, as well as all of this. It will all be OK.'

Sal sat across from me. His pale eyes were steady behind his glasses. 'One step at a time, Bavar, that's all you can do.' He frowned at my plate. 'Goodness. There's half a cow there!'

'It's good for him,' Aoife said. 'Nourishing.'

I pushed it away. 'No, thank you.'

She tutted and sat next to me, pouring the tea. 'We're with you, Bavar. Maybe not out there – but in here, we are all with you.'

There was a deafening roar as the portraits through the house responded to her. Cheers of 'Bavar!' and 'Our boy!' And Aoife smiled, and Uncle Sal buttered a piece of toast with his usual precision, and they meant well. They always mean well. But I sent the creature back with a strike of my hand, and so there will be more.

Aoife doesn't know quite what to say to me now. She can tell something's wrong, and she knows I'll only talk when I'm ready, so she's been baking all day, and not a bit of it looks like it'd be actually edible.

'Why did you say she was a catalyst?' I ask her, sitting at the kitchen table and picking crumbs off a blackened piece of something or other.

She gives me a long look. 'Because she shifted something in you. You're connected, somehow.'

'I don't see how we can be. Neither does Grandfather.'

She bristles at the mention of him. 'Well, perhaps he doesn't. But I'm fairly sure *you* know what I'm talking about, Bavar. Nothing has been the same since the day she started at your school, has it? That day you came back all hassled because she saw you just as you really are, you'd grown an inch! *She* did that. And she made you strike out last night, didn't she? Made you go out there in the first place, probably . . .'

'She was nothing to do with it!' I burst.

Aoife raises her eyebrows and turns back to her baking. I take a deep breath and try to wind myself back in. It's harder than usual. Everything is, since Angel came. And I know that makes Aoife right, but I don't really feel like saying that.

'I'm sorry,' I say eventually. 'About missing school. I'll go back, after the weekend.'

'It's all right,' she says after a while, sifting flour into an enormous bowl. The low winter sun shines through the kitchen window and catches all the copper pots hanging up above the counters. 'You have enough to deal with. I know the nights are getting harder. One day off school,' she raises her shoulders. 'I called them, told them you had a bug.' She looks up then with a funny little smile. 'You do have a bug, don't you?'

I don't know whether she means the raksasa or Angel. Or both. I shrug, and watch as she cracks eggs into the bowl, flinging the empty shells into the sink.

Angel saw me, up on the roof. She saw the raksasa, saw me strike out against it. And I don't know how to face her after that, catalyst or not.

Angel

There's always some fairly intense training involved in fighting supernatural creatures, I've seen the TV programmes. There are usually punchbags, and some running in the rain with music. I look at myself in the mirror – I don't look like one of those girls. I look a bit scrawny, and my hair is sort of floating around my shoulders in a frizzy static mist. But anyway. I've thought about it long and hard, since I saw Bavar up on the roof with that monster, and I figure this is what I'm here for. This is why I ended up with Mary and Pete, in this town. It was some kind of meant-to-be thing. I always told myself I would have fought them, if I could, and now here they are. So I'm going to help him, whether he likes it or not, and it starts today.

Actually, it was supposed to start first thing, in

that pre-dawn murky light, but I had an accidental lie-in, and then Mary cooked bacon and eggs, so now it's afternoon, but that's fine. Today is still the day. I put my headphones on, and my trainers, and tuck the catapult into my pocket, and I don't really have running gear as such, but I've got leggings and a hoody so I reckon that'll do.

'Going out?' asks Mary, coming out of the sitting room as I get downstairs.

'For a run,' I say. 'Is that OK?'

'It's fine,' she says with a smile. 'Actually, hang on ...' She goes to the kitchen and starts rummaging in a cupboard. I'm a bit surprised by the rummaging, to be honest – everything always looks so neat and tidy here. Anyway, she comes back eventually with a water bottle that has a hole in the middle. 'I bought it a few years ago,' she blushes. 'I thought I'd take up running.'

'And you didn't?'

'Don't have the right sort of knees, apparently.' She shakes her head and thrusts the bottle at me. 'Go steady out there. Looks like rain to me.'

'I don't mind that,' I say, opening the front door. 'Might be out a while; going to pop in on a friend.'

'Oh yes?'

I know she wants more, but I have no idea where I'd start, so I just pretend I didn't hear her and get out of there.

'Don't be late!' she calls out after me.

It starts to rain just as I get to the top of the road. I put my music on and head past the old, crumble-down church and up the hill, and for a while it's feeling pretty good, and I could almost be one of those girls in the movies, but the closer I get to Bavar's house, the wilder the weather gets, and black birds tumble in the sky over my head, shouting as they wheel about each other, and it all gets a bit spooky. I try to make myself head up the slope, but the house looms over me and it's not yellow in this murk, it's just a dingy shadow on top of the hill. When I look up I can see the ghosts of Bavar and the monster, from the other night. He's big enough to fight the nightmares. I *wish* I'd been that big.

I wish I hadn't hidden in the cupboard. More than anything.

Anything.

I stop, winded, and put my hands on my knees, looking up at the house, the backs of my eyes throbbing. Breathe. I can't change that now; all I can do is keep going. Keep breathing, keep moving, keep fighting. I have to know how it's all connected, who Bavar really is, and why the monsters are here. Why did they come to our house, that night? Why my parents? Was it because of Dad, and his work? Did he find the monsters, the ones that are here with Bavar? Did he somehow lead them back to our house? It's been there for a while now, that little niggle. Ever since I first saw Bavar, it's been getting stronger. What if it was Dad's fault somehow? What will I do then?

I put the thought to the back of my mind and stare up at the leaden sky, picture those great monsters circling the house. There must be a reason they come *here* – a reason Bavar was out on that roof. But he's not exactly forthcoming with stuff, so maybe I'll have to find out for myself. I stand there for a moment, looking from the house to the woodland that stretches out for miles behind it, and an idea comes to me. Instead of ringing that ridiculous doorbell, I'll just have my run through the woodland. I might stumble upon something, some old structure with strange symbols, maybe an ancient gardener who knows the family secrets. Or I could just find the back door, and sneak in by myself.

The wind howls and leaves spill like confetti from

the branches of the trees as I climb over a stout iron gate and trip through low branches, trying to find a path. Brambles catch at my clothes, and tangled roots stretch across the ground. It gets darker as I go, and there are shuffling, creeping noises that make my ears ring. I turn, but I can't see the way back. These woods are alive in a way that's not like any other wood I've been in. From every angle it feels like eyes are watching, creatures hiding. I push my way through the trees, faster and faster, until finally they open out into a damp, cold clearing.

I have no idea where I am, or where I'm heading. A little shiver winds up my spine, and my breath steams out in front of me. 'Which way now?' I ask in a whisper, turning and turning, hoping something will become familiar. As though in response, the air lights up with pale green sparks; fireflies, perhaps, that dance all around me and make the shadows retreat. I step forward as they dart ahead, and the trees make an archway over a narrow path. I hold my breath and tread as quietly as I can, and after a while the living things begin to show themselves: a rabbit, shuffling through the undergrowth; a white-tailed deer, making me jump as it leaps across the path; and then a pheasant, which waddles in front of me, feathers glowing green-white in the light of the fireflies. The dancing lights spin in the air in front of me, always just out of reach, and then the path opens out, and down a steep bank I pick my way over the roots of the trees and down, down to a cemetery, where a familiar figure crouches, his back turned to me.

'Bavar?' I whisper. He jumps up, the fireflies scatter, and now it's only the light of the moon, casting him all in silver.

Bavar

Nobody comes here.

Nobody ever comes here, and yet here she is. The fireflies scatter over our heads and a million points of light shine down on her, and I am sure there has never been another like her here in these woods, where all things are dark and hiding in the deep.

'Angel?'

'I came for a run,' she says, pushing her hair back, looking around her with wild eyes. 'And I thought I'd see the woods, and then the fireflies led me here. What is this place, Bavar?'

'It's the cemetery,' I say. 'That's all.'

'It's creepy!'

I look back at it as she steps further in, and I suppose maybe it is creepy, if you don't know it. But I grew up coming here, where it's quiet and everything rests, and I climbed the old yew trees that tangle overhead, and counted stars, and looked out over the town, watched the lights go out as night grew deeper. It always felt good here.

'It's not so bad,' I say. 'But you shouldn't be here.'

'Ah,' she says, walking around me, peering down at the ancient gravestones. 'But I should. Because the fireflies brought me here.'

'They're not known for their intelligence,' I say.

She looks at me and shakes her head. 'It's nature, Bavar. Nature brought me here. And I'm not going anywhere – not until I understand *everything*.'

I lean back against the crumbling stone wall and sigh. I guess I should have expected this. After the other night, she was bound to have questions. She always seems to have questions. I just don't know if I have the answers she wants. Either way, we're going to be here a while.

I watch her wander through the cemetery, and I know there's a reason she's here, beyond idle curiosity. That thing I catch in the corners of her eyes sometimes, that searching thing that has secrets, and knows about darkness nearly as much as I do. It needs something.

So, I remind myself, this is not friendship. But it's closer than I've ever been before, and it's not terrible to be here with her.

It's even a little bit nice, for now.

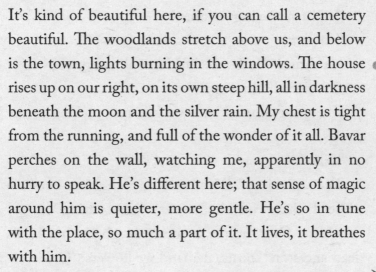

Angel

It's kind of beautiful here, if you can call a cemetery beautiful. The woodlands stretch above us, and below is the town, lights burning in the windows. The house rises up on our right, on its own steep hill, all in darkness beneath the moon and the silver rain. My chest is tight from the running, and full of the wonder of it all. Bavar perches on the wall, watching me, apparently in no hurry to speak. He's different here; that sense of magic around him is quieter, more gentle. He's so in tune with the place, so much a part of it. It lives, it breathes with him.

'So you have your own private cemetery,' I start, moving between the headstones. They're all of the same dark stone, in varying stages of decay. Soft green moss grows on some of them, lichen clinging to the lettering.

I try not to look too closely – I don't want him to think I'm being morbid – but I can't help noticing that most of these people weren't very old when they died. 'Is it just for your family?'

'Yes.'

'Do you look after the plants?' There are little pots of heathers and herbs, some of them with little white star-flowers that seem to glow against the darkness. 'What's this one?'

'Night-blooming jasmine.'

'It's pretty.'

He shrugs. 'Be trouble if I let it all get run down.'

'Trouble? From who?'

'Them, of course,' he says, his eyes flicking to the stones.

'Who?'

'We should go,' Bavar says, ignoring my question while I shake off the shiver that's sitting on my shoulders. Does he mean there are ghosts here? His dead ancestors' spirits, demanding flowers? 'Come on. It's not safe here.'

'Why not? What's here?'

He sighs. 'Nothing's *here*. I mean you need to get off the estate, before it gets any later.'

'But why?' I press, following him as he heads into the darkness of the trees. 'Bavar, slow down – just tell me what's going on here. What is this place? What *are* you?'

'What am *I*?' He stops and turns, and the sky seems to darken around us as we stand there, halfway up the hill. His hair is wilder than ever, standing out around his head in wiry coils. 'What's *that* supposed to mean?'

Oops.

'I didn't mean that,' I say, standing tall, about halfway up to his knees. 'I just . . . I'm sorry – I didn't mean that you were anything. I just need to know, about the monsters.'

'*Why?*'

'I know they're real,' I whisper. And I can't look him in the eye when I say it because I spent months trying *not* to believe in all of this. I fought every day just to believe in myself when everybody else told me I was wrong. And I *wasn't* wrong. Bavar takes a step away from me.

'How do you know?'

'I saw things, a while ago. And I saw you the other night, up on the roof. I saw you there, and you can't tell me that's not real, Bavar. You can't tell me I didn't see that, because I know I did, and I've had enough of pretending. I just need to *know!*'

He shakes his head. 'You *don't* need to know. You have no idea what you're trying to get into. You shouldn't even be here. You should be down there, in your nice safe little house, watching TV.'

My nice safe little house?

Breathe.

'You should stop acting like you're the only kid in the world who ever had to go through difficult stuff!' I burst. 'You have no idea about me, or what I'm capable of. You're just stuck up here in your mansion on top of the hill and you think you know it all and you think your life is oh so flipping difficult and it's just *not*, because you're seven feet tall and you could probably do *anything*, if you wanted to. So why don't you? Why don't you let people see you? Why do you spend all your time hiding – why don't you just *fight?*'

He stares at me a long time, while I try to stop the tears that want to come bursting out. It's raining hard now, and I didn't mean to lose it like that. I don't remember the last time I shouted at anyone.

'I don't want to fight,' he says eventually in a quiet voice. 'Everybody wants me to fight, and they all say the same thing. That I was built to fight.' He looks down at himself and then looks back at me, his eyes fierce. 'But I wasn't. And I won't.'

It gets darker, as I follow him through the tangled branches of the trees. The tall, narrow trunks glisten black in the dusk, rain streaming over everything. Bavar moves pretty stealthily, especially for someone of his size, and I slide around behind him, scrambling over the twisted roots that hide beneath a sodden layer of autumn leaves.

'Bavar?'

He stops, tilts his head, then carries on walking, harder, faster, completely ignoring me.

'Bavar!'

'Shhh!' He turns to me. 'They're already on our tail – why are you shouting?'

'What do you mean, *on our tail*?' I turn and look back, my teeth chattering. 'I can't see anything!'

'Look deeper,' he says, his voice a low, slow rumble that moves like thunder through the trees. 'Ahead, and to your right, under the elm.'

I can't tell an elm from a Christmas tree, but I look where he gestures, and deep down in the shadows is something that is *nearly* a badger. It's the same size, and it has the same stripes, but there's a spine of silver spikes down its back, and its coat sparkles like cut glass.

'What kind of creature is that?' I whisper, as it shuffles backwards with a high-pitched bark that makes my ears ring. Trees shudder around us, and there's a sudden silence. Bavar grabs at my arm and pulls me away, and we run, faster and faster, until my head is spinning, my breath burning in my chest.

'Bavar!' I wrench myself away, staggering to a stop. 'Don't do that! You can't just . . . you have to at least warn me when—'

'When what?' he asks, peering down at me. 'When I'm pulling you out of danger?'

'From sparkly badgers?'

He half smiles, shaking his head. He's breathing nearly as hard as I am, I notice with some satisfaction. Clearly the supersonic thing takes a toll on him too.

'You have to tell me, first.'

'OK.'

'And anyway, it didn't look dangerous. It was beautiful.'

'I never said it wasn't,' he mutters, trudging on

through the undergrowth. I follow him. 'But it's not just the badgers. There are lots of creatures in these woods. Bigger than that, more dangerous.'

I stare at his back for a long time, a word winding around inside my head.

'What?' he demands, turning.

'Magical?'

He returns my stare.

'It's that kind of place,' he says. 'Everything here . . . it's all affected.'

'By magic.'

He nods, his shoulders lifting.

'And that's why people don't see you. That's the thing, that makes you different?'

'That's part of it.'

He looks so uncomfortable. It's almost hard to see him, like he's getting smaller, disappearing into the shadows.

'Don't do that.'

'What?'

'You know what you're doing. It won't work. I see you. I saw you from the start.'

He frowns. 'Why? Why did you see me, when everybody else doesn't?'

'I told you, I saw stuff. I guess that makes me special now.'

'Aoife calls you my catalyst.'

'What does that mean?'

'I don't know. We're connected, somehow.'

'I don't know about catalysts . . .' I mutter. I don't really know about any of this, actually. Why *am* I here, in these spooky woods, with a monster-boy who smells of everything I was trying so hard to forget?

Because I can't forget it. And then there he was, in my face at school. He shakes his head as I stare at him, and then the clouds above us start to glow orange. The black silhouette of something monstrous appears, high up in the sky.

'We need to get out of here,' says Bavar.

The sense of power rings stronger than ever in the air around him. My instincts tell me to step back, get away, but I ignore them, my heart beating hard in my ears as the dark shape gets closer.

'What is that?'

'Run!' he hisses, grabbing me by the arm and pulling me with him, charging through the trees to the gate. A shuddering roar fills the air around us and I look up fearfully and realize it's Bavar. Bats rise with a flurry of panic as the creature gets closer, the flap of its wings bringing back memories I've been trying to hold at bay.

'Bavar!'

'I see it!' he shouts, pushing me behind him and stretching up as the monster gets closer. In an instant he is taller, broader. The creature flaps its wings, lowering its head to snap at us with vicious long teeth, and Bavar shouts as he reaches out. There's a brief, violent scurry, and I don't know whether it's the words he uses or just the sheer strength of him, but somehow he beats the monster back, and it peels away into the stormy sky with a screech of fury.

'What *was* that thing?' I ask after a while. My heart is thumping so loud, I'm surprised he can't hear it. He turns to me, still at full height, his eyes blazing. 'Has it really gone?'

I refuse to quail.

'For now,' he says, taking a deep, shuddering breath. He looks me up and down. 'But it'll be back. So thanks for that.'

'Why is it *my* fault?'

'Well, nobody else is running through the woods like a fairy princess!'

I look down at myself, in my muddy leggings and

the hoody that I outgrew about a year ago. 'I think you have the wrong idea about fairy princesses.'

'And you have the wrong ideas, generally,' Bavar says, rubbing at his face and seeming somehow to fold in upon himself, until he's plain, stooped old Bavar again. 'Why can't you just stay away?'

'I've told you. Because I can't. Because it matters.'

'What do you think you can do about it anyway?'

'I could fight!'

He shakes his head and starts to walk away, and I can't stand it, I can't take any more. I pull at him, and he turns back, his eyes wide with surprise. I guess he doesn't get pulled around a lot. 'I would fight,' I say, my chest tight with it. 'I *will* fight.'

'*Why?* And what if that's not the right thing to do? What if it makes a monster of you too?'

'I don't know. I guess I wouldn't care.'

'No, you wouldn't.' His eyes burn. 'You wouldn't care about anything. You'd be too far gone, on all your victories. You'd be a monster yourself, full of the fight and the kill and nothing else. No humanity left, you'd just spend your time celebrating, thinking how great you were, and then you'd make mistakes, and everything would go wrong . . .'

'But at least I'd have tried!'

'No!' he shouts. 'That's what they did. And then it *did* all go wrong, and there were consequences . . .' He shakes his head. 'There's a better way. There *has* to be a better way!'

'What are you talking about, Bavar? Who made mistakes? What consequences?' My heart skippers and twists and suddenly I don't know if I'm ready for this after all.

'Never mind,' he says in a heavy voice, staring at me.

'So what, then?' I demand. 'What's the answer? What's your *better way*?'

'I'm trying to work that out,' he says.

There's a rustle in the bushes behind me, something bursts out running, and I yelp, springing forward into him. Caught off guard, he stumbles down the bank and we both end up in a heap in the mud.

'What's *wrong* with you?' he howls, springing up and brushing off his backside, as a spotted deer bounces off into the darkness.

'It startled me!'

'The deer startled you?' he huffs, making for the iron gate. 'Monsters you can deal with, but one little deer and you're all screamy.'

'I was *not* screamy,' I say, following him, my eyes constantly searching the darkness for other things that might pop out. 'And it might have been some other kind of thing, and I might have just saved your life. So I think you could be a *bit* grateful.'

He glares back at me, and a strange expression crosses his face. I look down at myself, covered in mud, bits of twig sticking to me. When I look back he's already marching on, his shoulders shaking.

I think he might be *laughing*.

Bavar

'What on earth happened to you?' Aoife puts down her pen, her eyes wide. 'Is there trouble?'

'Definitely trouble,' I mutter, heading for the fridge and pulling out the milk as she pushes her crossword aside. She loves crosswords, her spidery handwriting fills dozens of them all stacked on the shelves by the table.

'You're getting mud everywhere!' she complains, standing as I get a glass out of the cupboard. 'What sort of trouble, Bavar – should I be worried?'

'No, it's fine. It's just the girl.'

'Your catalyst!' says Aoife. 'What has she been doing?'

'She came into the woods. Found me there, disturbed a bit of the wildlife, that's all.'

She was like a beacon in the gloom, as we trampled through the undergrowth, and shadows gathered thick and fast, and she didn't even see them. She didn't see the remnants of that other world that gather here, the bats and the half-bats and the lizards with fire on their tongues, she didn't hear how they called to the raksasa to come, come quick because *humanity is here*.

Why does she see me so clearly? Why does she want to fight? I believe her when she says it, there's a spark in her eyes, like she'd be happy just to lose herself in all this madness. But why? Is Aoife right? Is she really somehow connected?

'And the mud?' Aoife interrupts my thoughts, gesturing at my clothes.

'We fell into a boggy bit.'

'A boggy bit,' she repeats, her lips twitching. 'Well, I'm glad you were having fun out there.'

My cheeks get hot.

'You saw her safely away, though?' Her face grows serious.

'No, I left her wandering in the darkness.'

'Bavar!'

'Yes, I saw her safely away. She's fine. Also muddy.'

I finish the milk, put my glass by the sink. 'I need to get changed.'

'Bavar?'

'Yes?' I turn by the door.

'What's her name?'

I was kind of hoping not to have to tell them all. I know they'll make a song and dance about it.

'Angel,' I mutter.

'I beg your pardon?'

'Angel.'

Her eyes widen, and the whole house erupts with a chorus of 'ANGEL, ANGEL! BAVAR HAS FOUND AN ANGEL!' Every portrait shouts it, all my ancestors bright-eyed with it; they're insufferable, all the way up the stairs and down the corridor to my bedroom, where, fortunately, there are only paintings of ships.

Angel

'Angel, you have to get up!'

'It's Sunday,' I mutter into my pillow.

It's Sunday and I'm trying to get nightmares out of my head.

'And it's eleven, and so it's time to get up, young lady.'

There's a firmness in Mary's voice that wasn't there before. Like she knows me better now, since the crumpet-bonding exercise, so she's allowed to be stern. She's standing in the doorway, arms folded. She wasn't that impressed by the state of me when I got in last night; I was lucky to avoid a lecture.

'Cup of tea?' I wheedle.

'Yes, downstairs in five minutes,' she says, with a glimmer of a smile.

Hmph. I bet Bavar doesn't have to deal with this kind of thing. I try to imagine what it's like in that house. If the woods are filled with magical creatures, what sorts of things might live with him there? It's probably full of strange people: a butler, with horns on his head and hoofs instead of feet; a cook who's half horse – all of them there at his beck and call . . .

'Angel!'

No such luck here. I haul myself out of bed, put my jeans and a jumper on, and slither down the stairs. My bones feel exhausted; it's an effort just to get them to move. Mary hands me a mug of tea.

'Get some air,' she says. 'You look like you need it. Pete's doing some jobs outside, you can watch him.' She gives me a sideways look. 'Or even help . . .'

Too tired to argue, I plonk myself on the doorstep. It's a bright morning, the air is crisp and it clears my throat, cuts through all the heaviness. Pete nods when he sees me there, with a little smile. He doesn't say much, does Pete. He's wearing a hat, to keep the sun off his face, I suppose – though it's November, so that seems a bit unlikely. He's painting the fence a brighter shade of white. Maybe he doesn't want to get the paint on his head. He doesn't have much in the hair department.

He's so painstaking. After a while it starts to annoy me a bit. Up, down, neat straight lines, no rush, nothing but white paint, up and down.

'Want to help?'

I shrug. 'No?'

He nods and turns back to his work.

Oh for goodness sake.

'Haven't got painting clothes.'

'I have old shirts . . .'

Dad-sized shirts. Oh no. No.

A massive wave, heading in my direction, of Dad. Please no. Not today.

'Here,' says Pete, scrambling up and thrusting the brush in my hand. 'Screw the clothes, just do it.'

I'm too shocked to argue; I just do as I'm told. I paint until my wrist aches, until the cold is biting hard and there's paint everywhere. On my hands, on my clothes, on the grass, and all over his neat fence, in messy great loops and swirls.

'So, where did you get to yesterday, on your run?' Pete breaks in eventually.

I give him a look. He ignores it, keeps on painting.

'I was in the woods.'

'The old manor woods?'

'Yeah.'

'Strange place. I'm not sure I'd want to go running there alone.'

'I met a friend there . . . it was OK.'

'They used to have a lot of parties up there,' Pete says, halting in his work. 'I think they were fairly spectacular. Sometimes, when the wind was blowing the right way, you'd hear the music and the chatter, even here. I always wondered what it was like.'

'You never went?'

'No! They had people travel in, I don't know where from. We'd see them occasionally, driving through the High Street in enormous old cars. Very glamorous.'

'But they don't do that any more?'

'Not for a year or so.' He dips his brush in the paint. 'It's good that you have a friend here.' He hesitates, starts painting again. 'Don't forget, you have us too.'

I don't know what to say to that, so I attack the next fence panel, slapping white paint all over the place, wondering when he's going to tell me to be careful, or to stop ruining his garden. But he doesn't. After a while he fetches more tea and biscuits and we sit together on the step. I curl my brittle fingers around the mug and focus on just being here, breathing. Noticing the sky, the birds wheeling overhead. Pete, dunking a biscuit in his tea. Mika, winding around my ankles.

We never had a pet, at home.

'He likes you.' Pete smiles.

'He's not around much, is he?'

'He's a bit feral,' Pete says. He gives me a meaningful look, as if to say that's something we have in common.

Well. That's OK.

I stroke the cat. The cat purrs. And I make a little promise to myself: I'm going to help Bavar. I don't know what his life is like, in that house. I don't know why the monsters strike there, or how he's connected to what happened. I don't know why he's so scared of fighting. I just know that he seems more alone than even I am, right now, and so I'm determined. Whether he wants it or not, I'm ready for a fight. I'm ready to face the creatures there who tore my life apart.

Bavar

Awake. For a moment I don't know why. I stare into the darkness and listen to silence, and then a screech hits my spine. I scramble out of bed as Sal bursts in.

'The girl is outside the wall! She'll come in, Bavar!'

'The girl?' I swipe my robe from the chair by the bed, following him into the corridor.

'Your catalyst! If she gets in, Bavar . . . if it gets a smell of human blood!'

Angel.

'I'm going,' I whisper through clenched teeth, racing away from him, down the stairs, adrenaline coursing through me. There's no time to think, no time to hesitate. She's not the sort of girl to stay outside the wall if she's decided to come in.

The raksasa screeches as I fling open the front door

and run down the steps. It flurries over my head, its enormous wings rustling. I duck my head as it dives down, a red-skinned, furious creature that has stalked my nightmares and my night-time reality for as long as I can remember now. It fills the night sky, striving to break through the barrier to reach the girl outside the wall. I realize I can smell her blood. Her fear. I run towards the gate as she starts to scale the wall next to it, and by the time I get there she's pulled herself to sit on top of it.

The creature flies at her just as I reach the gate.

'Get down!'

The look on her face as I climb through brambles and reach up for her. She's just watching the raksasa, her eyes shining. Like she's daring it to come faster, come harder, because it's just what she was waiting for.

I pull at her arm and brace myself as she falls into me. The raksasa screeches and hurls itself at us, and I'm holding on to the gate with one hand, Angel with the other. I bend forward to shield us both with my back, and she slips through my fingers, landing lightly on her feet below me as the creature thrusts its claws into my robe, its wings beating either side of my face. I tear the robe away and the raksasa wheels up into the sky, screeching.

It's not done yet. I steady myself, turning on Angel.

'Go. Run!'

She steps up to me, her eyes flicking between me and the raksasa.

'No.'

'You're making it harder!'

She puts her hand on my chest.

'You have to fight!'

'No,' I push her away, towards the gate. 'Run!'

She staggers, falls. Looks up into the amber eyes of the raksasa, and howls.

Angel

The monster flies right at me. Oh, I know it's madness. I've flipped. Lost it. But I couldn't hear that sound in my dreams another night and do nothing. It's like I've been sleeping for a year, and now I'm awake, and it's electrifying. Bavar steps over me just as the thing gets within striking distance and puts his arm up to thrust it away. He seems to grow as he does it, as broad and long as the monster itself, shouting as he throws it on to the ground. Its wings beat against him and he bows his head, stretches up to the creature's neck. Something roars, I can't tell whether it's Bavar or the monster, the air sparks around them and then there's a massive *crack* and a new, absolute silence. An absolute stillness. The air rings with it.

In the darkness it's hard to make out the details.

Silhouettes of shapes. Of sinew and muscle, wing and outstretched arm. Slowly Bavar moves away, pulling himself on his elbows out of the tangle of limbs. He keeps his head low as he rises to a crawl, retching, making for the shadows at the edge of the garden.

'Bavar . . .'

He sits against the wall and tips his head back, stretching his legs out. I walk unsteadily, suddenly freezing, crouch by him. Watch tears roll down his cheeks. He doesn't move, doesn't speak.

I find his hand on the ground, put mine on top of it. It fits in his cold palm.

'I'm sorry.'

Bavar

Did I?

Did I have to? Was there another way? If she'd stayed behind the wall.

If I'd stayed in the house. Never gone to school.

My hands, around its neck. Hairless skin, like crumpled leather.

Crack.

It's so quiet now. The sky is so clear; a thousand stars bright above my shame. And it's cold, and I can't feel anything except her hand in my palm. So small. How can she put it there? How can she touch me now? Touch those hands, my hands, when they just did that? The raksasa lies stiff, a massive shadow over everything else.

It took an instant, that's all.

One moment, to make me the monster they've been asking for all this time.

Angel

I don't know what to do. I don't know how long we've been just sitting here while frost gathers around us. I can't move. There's this weird feeling, like if I take my hand away now, he'll be gone. I know it doesn't make sense; there's just something so unnaturally still about him, like he let go. I try not to look at the monster in the middle of the garden. For a second, in the heat of it all, it was hard to tell them apart. His roar, his rage was just as powerful as that of the creature he fought. Is that what he's been so afraid of? After a while I realize I'm just counting breaths; mine and his. They plume in the air, regular and soothing.

'Should we go in?' I ask, when the cold is biting deeper, and our breath is slower. 'It's too cold, Bavar . . .'

'What happened to you?' he asks in a whisper.

I look at him; his eyes are still on the sky. I get it – he doesn't want to look down, to see what he did.

'That happened,' I whisper, gesturing at the monster. 'One of those. It came for us.'

He whips away from me, rises to a crouch.

'What?'

I back away. I'm not sure he even heard me – his eyes are glazed, sick-looking. 'Bavar, we should go in; you need help.'

He looks down at himself, his clothes torn, skin scratched by the creature's claws. He looks at the monster. And then he looks at me, and starts to laugh.

Bavar

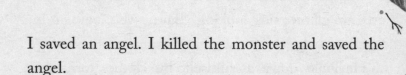

I saved an angel. I killed the monster and saved the angel.

She said something that made my blood run cold, but now I can't . . . I can't remember why. My jaw aches, my hands are throbbing, my stomach hurts, and there are a million little darts of pain over my skin where the raksasa's claws scored into me.

Aoife is running towards us and her mouth is moving, but I can't hear what she's saying. The girl stands, and they both stare down at me.

'Bavar, come!' Aoife demands. 'Who knows when the next will strike. You're in no condition to be sitting here just waiting for trouble.'

'What're we going to do with it, Aoife?' I ask, my eyes on the creature, a wave of nausea rolling in my stomach.

'Don't worry about that, just get in the house!'

I notice the girl, Angel, is coming too. Will she even be able to walk through the door of the monster house? How is all of this happening? How did the world change so fast? It spins around me as I head up the steps, as I watch her disappear into the light ahead of me. I feel myself falling, catch myself on hands and knees, head for the light, the clamour of the house.

They're howling.

All the ancestors in all their heavy frames. Howling, hooting, crowing, as I crawl into the house. They think I'm the victor; they think I've come into my own. And here I am on my knees, while the world spins, and the angel comes at me as I kick the front door shut, and so I lower my head because I've seen enough. Enough, enough, enough.

Angel

I know how to cry. I know how to be small. I know how to curl myself up on the inside so none of me shows, and nothing can hurt. Being in this house is like the opposite of that. It's dark, and the air sparks, like danger might be just around the corner. But it's so *alive*, it's like sunshine in my veins, like magic spinning through the air, fine as dust, and I'm breathing it in and there's something growing from the inside, something I didn't know I had any more.

I can see from the look in Bavar's eyes that he wishes I wasn't here. I guess maybe I'd feel like that too, if I was him. The woman walks ahead of us, her feet quick and light, and I linger at the doorway next to him. The hallway is vast, tiled in black and white, and a grand staircase sweeps up into the gloom. Chandeliers swing at regular intervals, but they seem to create shade as much as light, and then there are the portraits. Dozens, hundreds of them – all different sizes and shapes, and all of them, *all of them* looking at me.

They were shouting, a moment ago – I'm sure I didn't imagine it. They were shouting, cheering, as we came in.

Did I imagine it?

The woman stops and turns.

'I'm so sorry,' she says, her voice bright and a little breathless as she rushes back to me. Her hands are warm on mine, her smile lights up her narrow, pale face. 'We haven't met. I've heard of you, but perhaps Bavar hasn't told you of me, or of the house . . .' She gives a couple of the portraits a stern glance. There's a weird, stretched silence in the air, as if something's about to explode. 'I'm Aoife, Bavar's aunt. I'm sure you know, of course you've seen . . . this is a rather unusual place. The ancestors are all rather keen to meet you . . .'

I smile back at her, but I think I may have broken Bavar and I didn't think, I didn't realize it would be so hard for him. Aoife frowns, going to him as he feels his way along the wall, and I don't know what to do. I want to tell him it's OK, but I don't think it is OK – not for him. I pushed him to fight, and now his face is all shadows.

'Your first fight,' Aoife says, putting her thin arm around him. 'You did so well. You'll be fine, my love; it's just a shock to the system . . . Come, both of you. Hot tea, and a bit of toast. You'll be fine. This is good. It is a good day –' she looks back at me, her eyes shining – 'and we are very pleased to have you here, Angel.'

'ANGEL!'

The silence breaks, the house shudders around us and they call my name, from every wall, and every darkened crevice.

'ANGEL IS HERE!!'

Aoife cajoles me along, one arm still around Bavar, through wood-panelled corridors lit with little tasselled wall-lamps. The carpet is a maze of green and gold beneath my feet, and the portraits sing loudly of brave heroes and angels and monsters in the sky. It's kind of a relief when Aoife leads us into an enormous kitchen, bright and warm and silent – completely devoid of portraits. She notices me looking.

'I can't be having the ancestors in here,' she says. 'This is where I come to have a break from it all!' Bavar slides on to one of the chairs, looking exhausted, and

Aoife indicates for me to sit next to him. The chairs were clearly made for giants like Bavar, and so is the table. I feel like a little kid again, my feet swinging above the floor.

'Are you OK?' I whisper to Bavar, watching Aoife fill the vast copper kettle, and saw great slices of bread from a loaf on the side. His eyes follow her as she moves about.

'I don't know.'

'Bavar . . .'

He looks at me. His eyes are bloodshot.

'I'm sorry,' I say, and my voice wobbles. 'I really, honestly meant to help you. I was picturing you here, all alone, hiding from them, and I know how that feels and I didn't want you to feel like . . . like you didn't have help . . .'

'So you helped.'

I bite my lip. 'Yeah. I didn't realize what it would be like for you. I didn't mean to make it worse.'

He told me, didn't he? He told me there was a better way; he didn't want to fight. He didn't want to be a monster, past caring. Is that what he thinks he is now?

The toaster pops, making us both jump. Aoife reaches into a rack for plates, and starts clattering things down

127

on the table. I wince for him, as he puts his head in his hands.

'What do we do now?' I ask.

'Now?' He lifts his head, stares at me. 'I don't know what happens now. I've never killed before. What does happen, after you kill a thing?'

'You're still you!' I protest. 'You still care, don't you? You did all that *because* you cared, and you haven't suddenly grown horns, or anything! You were just . . .'

'Just what?' he demands. 'Just fighting? Just killing?'

'You didn't kill the raksasa,' says Aoife, coming back to the table with a steaming brown teapot. 'You merely sent it back to its own world; their bodies are only loosely connected with their spirits. It would take a lot more than that to kill one on the spot. You're not there yet, Bavar!' Her face softens as she sees the impact of her words on him. 'All you have done is send it back, where it can do no harm to anybody. One day, in your mastery, you will be able to deliver the world of them entirely, but that will only be when you are at your full strength.'

He melts back into the chair, hands falling to his sides, and I'm so *relieved* that I can't think of anything to say.

'They're called raksasa?' I ask eventually.

'It means *monster* in Indonesian,' Aoife says. 'Now, enough. Here is toast.' She passes me a plate and a knife. There's a dish of pale butter, and the toast is hot and truly about the size of a regular doorstep, so I dig in, but Bavar ignores it all.

'I need to close the rift,' he says, after a while.

'You can't,' Aoife says, shaking her head as she pours the tea.

'I don't want to do this every day. I need to close it. Grandfather says there's a way—'

'No,' she cuts him off. 'You're not making sense. You are what you are; this place is what it is. Not all things can be changed – some of them we must just adapt to.'

'But I'm not my mother, or my father. And you said if I went to school, I could be different.'

'Be different, yes!' she says, sitting across from him and looking him in the eye. 'Be centred, be wise. Be as human as you can be, for it is your humanity that can withstand the call of the magic that corrupted your parents. Go to school, have friends, learn to laugh a little, even, but there is no doubt about this one thing. You were born to fight them, Bavar. It is your duty, and you've only just begun.'

He lays his head on the table, and I wish she hadn't said that. It doesn't feel right, to make him do what he doesn't want to. Even if part of me still wants him to. Even if I think he's the greatest thing I've ever seen. I wish I could fight like that. I wonder if he ever saw the way it changes him. The way his whole body seems to come alive, shining bright. I wonder if he knows that it isn't all dark and evil; that when he's fighting, he's living harder than I ever saw anybody live, and it shows in his eyes.

'But—'

'Bavar, that's enough. We have company,' Aoife says. 'Let me get out that cake. I made a lovely chocolate cherry one; the sugar will do you good. And it's Uncle Sal's favourite, so he'll come and join us, and you can meet him, Angel.'

Bavar groans, his head still on the table, and she shakes her head as she pulls a great glass dome towards us, a mountain of dark something inside. She lifts her head and calls out, 'SAL! CAKE!' and Bavar sinks even lower in his seat, and I feel sorry for him, but also I can't help it – I LOVE THIS. She's so weird, the cake is so gruesome, and Uncle Sal, when he comes in, is such a contrast to it all. He's small and round and balding, with thick black-framed glasses, and the expression on his face isn't exactly kindly, but he's about as scary as pudding, and somehow, even after everything that just happened, and even though I'm worried about Bavar, somehow these three people make me smile on the inside.

Bavar

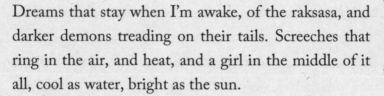

Dreams that stay when I'm awake, of the raksasa, and darker demons treading on their tails. Screeches that ring in the air, and heat, and a girl in the middle of it all, cool as water, bright as the sun.

Why does a human girl want to wade into a storm like that? Did she say? She said something, but it won't come to me now. It dances in tatters and won't come clear.

She didn't run.

She came into the monster house and she smiled. She looked around as if she'd never close her eyes again, and she smiled when her name echoed around the house, and I don't know what's going on any more.

It was simple, before. I was going to hide, and the raksasa were going to get bored and go home, and I was going to just be here, just quietly, and sometimes that seemed like a terribly lonely thing, but it was safe, and I wouldn't make mistakes with the barrier – I'd keep it strong, always – and after a while the raksasa would leave us alone, and now we've ruined everything. Now I'll be just like my parents were, before they left me here. I'll be a monster of a different kind; a monster who will lose his humanity and live for the fight and the glory of the win, past caring for anything else.

The ancestors sang a racket about an angel who they don't understand is actually just a girl with bright hair, and I never saw a smile like that before. So I don't think she's about to go anywhere. She never retreated and she never would have. I saw from the look on her face. That expression, I've seen it before. On my mother's face, as she went into battle.

That's how this place changes you. Over time, little by little, so you don't even really notice. Skin harder, brighter; blood stronger. And then more, more – I don't know when it happened, not exactly, but one day I looked at her and she was barely there at all. Her blue eyes glinted with silver, her teeth were sharper, in some lights they looked just like jagged points. They fought their monsters, held their parties, and when we did go

133

into town, there was a feral, wild look in my father's eyes that frightened me, like he just saw animals. He stopped hunching, rose to his eight-foot height and the air around him rang like a bell, deafening, and nobody saw us. The magic was too powerful; it was a mirror that they held between us and the real world. But I always wanted to be seen. That's why I agreed to go to school. To be part of it all. I just never expected it to actually happen. For anybody to really truly see me, just as I am.

'They see me now,' I say out loud. 'Now that Angel is there. She muddles it all up . . .'

There's no answer. I'm talking to myself. Aoife comes, and goes, and then she tells me the raksasa is gone. They crumble to dust in the light of dawn, like they never were. But the scratches are real, burning on my skin. I tell her they suit me, and Aoife gives me a despairing look.

'You saved her, Bavar! You saved her, stopped that creature from doing harm, and still you hide here? Still you hide from what you are?'

'Yes,' I tell her. 'Thank you, yes.'

She shakes her head and I know that however hard she tries to reassure me, deep down she's afraid I'll be just like them. Despite school, Angel, everything else, she's afraid that eventually I'll be a fighter, before anything else, and long after everything else is gone.

'Where were you hurt?' she demands.

'I'm fine.'

'Bavar, stop it. If you were scratched, we have to deal with it.'

'Deal with it. Yes.'

She mutters about poison and medicine, and how my body will get used to it in time, as I grow in power and strength, as I fight more of them.

'No,' I say. 'No thank you.' I sit up, visions of brightness dancing in front of my eyes. 'Did you see the angel? Where did it go?'

She leans in, touches my face. And then she huffs and goes to see Grandfather. She never goes to see Grandfather. She spent a lot of the time he was alive avoiding him and she always says she's not going to go courting a bronze statue, thank you very much.

But off she goes, muttering. Like, to be a fly on *that* wall.

The stuff in the cup is bog-green and it smells awful. Aoife is urging me to drink it, but there's no way.

'There is a way,' I tell her. Her eyes are bright, and light sparkles all around her in little swimming points. 'Grandfather said there is. There's a door to the rift . . . the door, and they opened it . . . and so it can be closed.'

I'm sure I remember him saying something about a door. I can't get it straight in my mind though; everything else is in the way. I bat the cup away and the green stuff splatters on the carpet.

'Bavar, you're not making any sense at all,' she says, and her voice is tired and it sounds like it cares but it wants me to fight, so I lie down because it's confusing and hot and I don't understand.

'The raksasa are interlopers,' says the face in the curls of the flocked wallpaper. 'A long time ago, before we knew better, we used our magic recklessly, and we opened the rift between our world and theirs. The raksasa had never smelt humanity before, and they craved it, terribly. We have been defending the world against that rift ever since; we use our magic to keep a barrier between our land and the rest of humanity. And when they come, we fight, because we must, and we have evolved to be so good at it! Aren't you pleased, Bavar, to have such a legacy?'

'No,' I say. I pull the pillows over my head, but the words keep ringing in my ears: they were Grandfather's words, a long time ago, when my parents were still here, and lessons were just lessons, and didn't mean me.

Angel

I see it, that night. Over and over again, the way he fought the monster. In the moonlight, how his skin gleamed.

It's a good vision; better than the usual by about a million per cent. And when I sleep, the dreams aren't the same. Yes, there are monsters. There's screaming, fear. But also there's Bavar.

So you know, a little bit of hope. In a hopeless place. If only he could see it.

Up close, they're so big. The smell, the unnatural heat in the air. That almost-human face, and the burning amber eyes that are as inhuman as you could get. I can't believe I launched myself at it.

What would Bavar have done, if I wasn't there?

Crouched, hidden in the house? Would he have let them beat him in the end? Would he have let them escape? Is that what happened, that night? I knew that house was connected with what happened to Mum and Dad. Same smells, same magic, same monsters. Now I'm wondering if his family had something to do with that night. Did someone slip up, let one of those creatures escape? Didn't Bavar say something about a mistake? And somehow it chose our house, all the way over in the city. The thoughts trip me from sleep and won't let me rest. Why us? Was it Dad's research that led them to us somehow? It can't all be a coincidence.

I remember the first time I saw Dad's business card: *Historian, Researcher into the Occult.* I thought it was all legend and fable, that he travelled the world collecting stories. But it was more than that, he was finding actual monsters. Was he researching Bavar's house? Did the monsters track him from there?

Did Dad lead them to our house?

'No,' I whisper, but his voice is silent in my mind and there's a horrible falling feeling deep in my chest. I thought we were victims. Innocent. But if he somehow led them to us, then it was his fault, wasn't it? *His* fault they're gone now.

'No,' I say, louder. He'd never put us in danger. But also, he'd never leave a mystery alone. And if he saw that boiling sky, and he knew what it meant, he wouldn't be able to help himself. I tussle with it all until my head aches, and then Mika bats at the door with his paw, and I let him in, and then we sit together and watch the sky brighten.

'Another day,' I whisper, stroking him between his ears. He lifts his head, purring. 'I guess you'll be out hunting, or lazing around. No school for *you* today, lucky thing.'

Somehow I can't imagine Bavar will be there either.

He looks terrible.

I don't know what I'm doing in his *bedroom*. I'm pretty sure he wouldn't be very happy about it if he was in his right mind.

Which he's not. Which is very unnerving.

I came straight here after school, all keen for answers, and finally plucked up the courage to use that awful bell, which does ring like the world's about to end. Aoife smiled as she opened the door and said she'd been waiting for me. She shoved the cup in my hand, and told me Bavar needed to drink it, whether he wanted to or not, and she was very sorry to put it all on me, but she'd been trying all day and now the situation was a bit critical. She brought me up the wide stairs, past all the curious faces in all the portraits to his room, which is about the size of a football pitch, and now here I am, and I don't know what to do.

'Bavar?'

He stirs, and pulls himself up. 'Angel!'

His eyes glitter, his cheeks are flushed. Aoife said it was the raksasa; apparently the poison in their claws isn't a problem when you're 'seasoned', but it can kill, if you've never encountered it before, hence the green stuff. Bavar spies it and wrinkles his nose, trying to get away from me. I'm perching on the edge of the bed, which is a bit like a forest-world all of its own, with its green vine curtains and about a million blankets and bedspreads. Heavy rugs overlap on the carpet, and a low fire burns in the grate. No wonder he looks hot. I push a few of the blankets on to the floor.

'Aoife says you have to drink this,' I say, holding the cup out.

'There's a rift – did you know?' he asks, his eyes wide, like a kid who just saw snow for the first time. 'My ancestors opened it, back in time,' he waves his hands in the air. 'They were playing with magic – spells from far-off lands. Then . . . then the monsters came through the rift and we made a barrier, to stop them reaching the rest of the world, but still they come, and so we fight them, we send them back.'

'Oh.' My mind races. I guess it makes sense. As much as any of this makes sense. 'But drink this . . .'

He pulls a face. 'Nope. So anyway. The rift. Grandfather says it's growing – all the time, growing. More 'n' more monsters'll come, in time. So I'm'a'find it. Close it.'

'Close the rift?'

'Yup. It's here somewhere,' he gestures widely. 'There's a door, a *hidden* door. So I'mma find it, and close the rift. No more rift, no more raksasa!' He grins.

It's kind of wicked, that grin. Makes me smile.

'I'll help you,' I say, wondering if there really is a door – a rift – that we could close.

He nods, and then turns pale. He really does look sick.

'You have to drink this first though,' I say, using my best commanding voice. Mum had a good one of those. I always knew, when I heard it, there'd be no arguing with that.

'Why?' he complains, scowling at it.

'It's . . . finding-hidden-door juice.'

His face brightens. 'Just what we need!'

'Yes.'

'You have some too.'

Oh my goodness.

'OK.'

I take a mouthful. It's about as vile as a thing can be, and it stays there, in my mouth, like a living animal. I take a breath through my nose, and swallow.

'There. Now you,' I say, trying not to retch. 'Drink it all, and we'll find this door . . .'

He tips his head back and drinks, and he *trusts* me, which makes a little rush of something go through me, and I don't know if I just did the right thing, but I know Aoife was pretty desperate about him, and I'm pretty sure he wants to live, after all.

He gasps, falling back on to his pillows.

'Bavar?' I lean forward. 'Are you OK?'

'That's terrible,' he mutters.

'I know! I'm sorry; Aoife said you needed it . . .'

'Probably.' He drags himself up, shuddering. 'I don't know why they have to make these things taste so disgusting though. Why can't they be like chocolate, or ice cream? Why do they always have to taste like toads?'

'You've had many of these things? You've eaten *toads*?'

'Had a few mishaps in the woods over the years.' He grimaces. 'And no, I haven't eaten toads. I reckon they'd taste like that though –' he gestures at the cup – 'Pretty vile . . .'

He looks a little less sick, I realize. Already, he's a better colour. I'm so relieved, I almost don't want to hassle him about the big stuff.

Almost.

Bavar

The buzzing has stopped, and it's like colour has come back into the world, only I hadn't noticed it'd gone away in the first place. The walls aren't talking to me any more; my heart isn't racing. I take a deep breath.

Angel's in my room.

'Why are you here?'

'I came to check on you. Good job, by the way; you wouldn't drink that stuff for Aoife.'

'But I did for you . . .'

'I tricked you.' She grins. And then grimaces. 'Had to have some myself first, mind. Anyway –' she brushes it away with a careless hand – 'now you're better. And I want to know –' she leans in, her eyes glowing – 'where's that rift we're going to be closing? You said something about a *door*?'

145

How does this keep happening when she's around? How does she always manage to get right to the heart of it, almost before I get there myself? And here I am, in *bed* of all places, and she's sitting there happily, as if everything's just brilliant and as it should be, talking of things she *definitely* shouldn't even *know* about.

'Shall we ask your grandfather?' she chirps. 'Where is he? I haven't met him yet . . .'

Of course, she doesn't realize that he's not exactly human any more. I smile.

'You want to see him?'

She nods, and slides off the bed, making for the door. 'Can we do it, Bavar?' She turns, her eyes bright. 'Close the rift; make them go away forever?'

That look. That hope. My head's still heavy, and I'm probably not quite myself yet, because I find myself nodding.

'We can try.'

Angel

Oh my goodness, his grandfather is a *statue*. He doesn't even have a body. He's a head, and a bit of chest, on a great big gleaming metal column thing.

'Are you trying to be funny?' I demand, as Bavar turns, holding a really horrible tablecloth in his hand, a grin on his face.

'Angel, Grandfather. Grandfather, Angel.' He gestures, with a bit of a bow.

'After all that, I thought we were getting somewhere, Bavar! I thought we were going to . . .'

'Angel,' the bronze head chimes. 'So, this is the girl.' He stares at me. 'You have caused quite the commotion here.'

I stagger back into the wooden table and perch on it, staring at the bust and then at Bavar. He's just about bouncing with delight, which is such a novelty it almost makes me smile.

Almost.

Come on, Angel, I tell myself. What did you expect in a house where the portraits howl, and poisoned boys are revived by green sludge?

'Pleased to meet you,' I say. My voice is a bit high, but he doesn't know what it normally sounds like.

Bavar does. He grins again, and I glare at him.

'So the two of you have been having adventures,' says Bavar's grandfather. 'I'm glad to see you are somewhat restored, Bavar. You know, your aunt was MOST ANIMATED about it.'

'She says he should fight,' I say.

'So he should – quite right.' The bronze nods.

'But he wants to close the rift.'

Bavar gapes at me, which is pretty enjoyable.

'Oh, does he?'

I fold my arms, and we both look at Bavar.

'Yes,' he says eventually, his shoulders hunched. 'You said there was a way.'

'And Angel here is going to be HELPING you?'

Bavar spreads his hands. 'Yes?'

'I see,' the bronze says. 'Well, I suppose a person

should have an accomplice. A brother in arms, if you will.'

'A *sister* in arms,' I correct him.

'A catalyst, Aoife calls you,' he murmurs, his bronze eyes gleaming as he looks at me. 'How did you fall into all this, my dear?'

'I don't know,' I say, which is sort of half true. I don't *know*. But I do know that if there's a way of stopping anyone else from being attacked by those monsters I want to find it. And if Dad was connected to it all, then so am I. And it's not like anybody else is getting things done. Most of the world doesn't even *see* what's going on here.

'The way will be long and hard,' Grandfather intones. 'And only the true shall *ever* find the real path . . .'

I catch Bavar rolling his eyes.

'I saw that, young man,' he huffs. 'You must find the DOOR. It's been hidden. Find the door, and you will find the rift. And then the real work will begin.'

'The real work?'

'CLOSING the RIFT!'

Bavar flinches. 'How do we do that?'

'You do that by first finding the door,' he says in a smooth voice. 'That is the first step; without it you cannot take any further.'

'Where is it?' he asks.

His grandfather shrugs, a shiver of bronze movement. 'No idea. In the house somewhere. Never seen it.'

Bavar sighs. 'Did you never look?'

'I always meant to,' he says, his voice softer. 'I thought there would be more time.'

'Well, it can't be that hard to find!' I venture. 'I mean, you say it's in the house, so it's right here somewhere.'

They share a look of amusement.

'Have you *seen* the size of this house?' Bavar demands. 'And besides, it plays tricks. We could be searching forever.'

'Oh,' I say. 'I guess we'd better start then. Maybe you should put some clothes on first?'

The bronze bust lets out a squawk of laughter, and Bavar looks down at himself. He is wearing various layers of robe, to be fair, but it's not exactly what I call dressed for an adventure. He huffs and throws the tablecloth back over his grandfather, who mutters darkly before going quiet.

'When shall we start?' I ask in a hushed voice as we head out of the library.

'You're serious?' He turns to me. 'You're really doing this?'

'*We're* doing it, aren't we?'

'But why?' he demands suddenly, stopping short and turning on me. His voice is an animal growl, and the narrow landing over the stairs darkens in an instant, cobwebs swinging over our heads. The back of my neck prickles and I can't help stepping back into the wall, away from him. 'Why are you doing it?'

'Because you weren't about to,' I say, trying to find my voice, my heart, as he stares down at me.

'Why does it matter to you so much?'

'Why wouldn't it?' I ask. 'How could I see you – see all this – and just walk away?'

'I don't know,' he breathes. Shadows cling to his face as he folds himself back into the corner, and for a second I can feel it, thick as the magic around him, all the loneliness, the hurt he carries.

'I'm not going to,' I say, stepping forward, making my voice strong. 'So you have that. Even if you don't believe in anything else. I'm not going anywhere, while all this is going on. We can do this, Bavar. I know we can.'

He shakes his head as we head down the stairs, and

I steady him when he stumbles.

'Tomorrow,' I say. 'We'll do it tomorrow, when you're better. And wearing proper modern-day clothes . . .'

'You said something last night,' he says, peering at me. He's flushed, and I realize he doesn't remember what I told him, after he fought the raksasa, about my parents. I can't bring myself to add to his misery right now.

'A lot happened last night.'

Aoife meets us as we get to the bottom of the stairs, looking us up and down. 'Bavar, how are you feeling?'

'I'm fine,' he says, brushing her away.

'It was nice of Angel to come by,' she says. 'You need a friend, Bavar.' She turns to me. 'Will you be back?'

'I could pop in after school tomorrow,' I say. 'We can finish that homework . . .'

'OK,' Bavar mumbles.

'Will you be at school?'

'Probably,' he says.

'Maybe it would do you good,' I say. And I do mean it. But also, I don't want him lingering around here all day, getting bored, thinking about secret doorways and rifts. He might do it without me. And obviously that would probably be a really good idea, because he's the one who has the magic, but I think I need it as much as he does. Maybe even more.

'I'll be there,' he says, staring at me as if he knows exactly what I'm thinking.

It's kind of creepy, walking down the path to the gate. The sky is quiet now; the air freezing. When I look back, the house is ablaze against the murk of dusk, lights shining from every window. You'd never know what went on here last night. You'd never even suspect. And it's funny. I came looking for answers, and I even got some, but that's not the thing that stays in my mind, as I go through the gate and down the hill. The raksasa are important, and finding the rift is important, what happened to Mum and Dad . . . that never leaves me. But right now, the thing that stays closest is the way he trusted me, when he was lying there all poisoned.

That, and the way his ancestors shouted my name. Never going to forget a whole house of portraits calling out at you like that, are you?

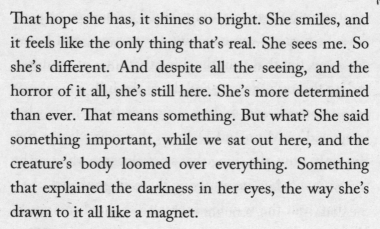

Bavar

That hope she has, it shines so bright. She smiles, and it feels like the only thing that's real. She sees me. So she's different. And despite all the seeing, and the horror of it all, she's still here. She's more determined than ever. That means something. But what? She said something important, while we sat out here, and the creature's body loomed over everything. Something that explained the darkness in her eyes, the way she's drawn to it all like a magnet.

Why can't I remember?

She gives a little wave as the gates swing open for her, and I catch that gleam in her eye, and so I know. We're doing this. We're looking for the rift, so that we can close it. I always thought I was the only one linked to it all, and now she's here, for whatever reason, and she's on a mission. She said she wasn't going anywhere while all this is going on, and so it almost felt true when Aoife said she was a friend. But when the mission is done, she'll go back to her own house, and this place will feel bigger, darker than ever.

And I'll be alone again.

Aoife is waiting for me when I close the front door. She's standing by the stairs, looking like she wants to talk, but my head is full of too many things, and none of them make sense, so I dodge her, escaping into the drawing room and finding myself before the mirror. Warped old glass in a pitted, age-darkened silver frame, stretching from the heavy stone mantelpiece nearly to the ceiling.

But that's not what catches my eye.

There, in the mirror. For an instant, the nearly-me, the could-be-me, straight and tall and just like any old boy with gnarly hair. But even as I look, he is surrounded by the shadows of everything I have tried so hard *not* to be: the monsters of my parents, and of every ancestor before them, gathered thickly around me, their faces glowing with pride as they reach out to me.

'I don't want to be like this. Like you,' I whisper, as

the image shifts and my sharpened teeth glint in the mirror.

'But you are,' they say. 'You already are. You always have been. Our Bavar!'

'Your monster.' I close my eyes, and that's almost worse, because now I can feel them, their energy hot in the air around me, the hot iron tang of their blood.

'What is a monster?' My mother's sibilant voice right next to my ear, her breath making my shoulders flinch. 'Something different? Something out of place? Many monsters in the world wearing their differences on the inside, dangerous people. You are the gatekeeper. You will protect these ordinary people from evils they have not dared to dream of.'

'Evils like you . . .'

'Sometimes it corrupts.' She shrugs. 'Sometimes in order to fight the worst, we have to understand them.'

'I don't want that.'

I don't want Angel to see me like that.

'Then don't do it. Stay true to yourself. Be better than me. Look at me, Bavar.'

I look up, and in the mirror it's just me and her. She

156

barely reaches my shoulder. When did that happen? When did she get so small? She smiles, revealing her own pointed teeth.

'You are my boy. My Bavar. You can do this. Do it your way, but do it. There are worse things in the world than anything you can ever become. And if you do not become what you should, then those things will win . . .'

I don't tell her about our plan. I'm pretty sure she'd just tell me it's impossible to close it, and I don't want her doubt to join my own. I need to believe in it, like Angel does. My mother hisses as I turn away, and I close my mind to her.

There was a time she wasn't like that. A time when she was softer, warmer, when she laughed, and held me. It's hard to hold on to those memories when I'm surrounded by the evidence of what they have all become, in this house. After a time, it does corrupt. That part that was human becomes something else. Something hard and bitter. Something dark. Features shift, bodies stretch, and hearts harden.

Now something else has changed. Angel has been here, and she's changed everything. The raksasa strikes its claws against the barrier that night, howling to be released into the world, and my ancestors roar. They want me to fight like I did last night, but I don't. I won't. I pull the curtains around my bed, and hold on tight for tomorrow.

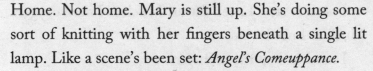

Angel

Home. Not home. Mary is still up. She's doing some sort of knitting with her fingers beneath a single lit lamp. Like a scene's been set: *Angel's Comeuppance.*

'You don't want to be here,' she says.

I look around, my stomach tight. I don't know if I'll ever get used to this house, the sounds and the smells so different from what I had before. I know it's not a bad place. I know they're kind, and I should be grateful.

'Not really.'

A twist of her mouth; a nimble dance of fingers.

'What shall we do?'

She's asking me. She's serious. Her brown eyes flicker, and she sets the knitting aside.

'We wanted to help, Angel.'

My name rings and doesn't sound right in this

vanilla house, with the tribal masks that they probably got from a cheap furniture shop. We had stuff from real places – Morocco, Italy, places we'd been. It's in storage now. I flinch away but she stares at me, determined.

'We don't want to make it worse for you. Is it worse, being here?' Her voice falters. She clears her throat. 'If you'd like us to contact them, make other arrangements . . .'

'No!'

I need to stay. I need Bavar. Much as I need oxygen. Much as I need water.

I need to stop the monsters.

'So,' she says with a deep breath. 'So stay.' She smiles. 'Stay. Go to school. Come home to us. Can you do that, every day?'

I perch on the arm of the settee.

'I have a friend. Sometimes I'll go there. To see him.'

'Him?'

'He helps.' I shrug.

'How do you know him? From before?'

'No. He's at school. He's . . . He doesn't fit.'

'Like you.'

She sees me. I nod. I can't speak right now.

'So. You have to tell me before you go out. And

160

where you're going. And what time you'll be home. You're thirteen, Angel. It's young, even with everything you've been through. You are still young. And I can't . . .' She shakes her head. 'It isn't the same, I know. But I do care.'

'I didn't ask you to.'

She smiles. 'I know. That bit wasn't up to you.'

I don't know how that makes me feel, so I just sit there for a while, watching the gold clock on the mantelpiece. It has little balls underneath that move constantly, rotating first one way then the other.

'Go on, it's bedtime,' Mary says eventually, patting my knee before picking up the knitting again. 'Try to get some sleep.'

'OK.'

Mika winds his tail around my ankles as I go up the stairs, and I pick him up – mainly to stop him from tripping me, but also because I suddenly have a desperate need to hold on to something alive and warm.

'Hey,' I whisper, gathering him close. 'How're you doing?'

He makes a funny little chirruping noise and puts his chin on my shoulder, his whiskers prickling at my ear. When we get to the top of the stairs I put him down, and he stalks into my bedroom, curling up on the end of the bed.

'Huh – and Pete says you're feral.' I smile, pulling the curtains and turning on the lamp. 'I guess he got that wrong. Or *maybe* –' I reach out and stroke him – 'you were just waiting for the right person . . .'

Bavar

She twinkles at me, all the way through school. Every classroom, every corner I turn, there she is, restless, almost humming with it.

'Why are you so into this?' I ask, while she steals all the extra little things Aoife put in my lunch, in case I wanted to share it with my new friend. There are cheese straws, weird prawn things, chocolate mints, and some kind of fruit that looks like a tiny yellow plum. 'Why does it matter so much to you?'

'Reasons,' she says around a mouth full of chocolate, avoiding my eye. 'I told you the other night. I'm not about to get into it all again now.' She pulls a bag of crisps from her lunch and opens it out so that the silver foil is like a tray. 'Help yourself. Salt and vinegar.'

'They're terrible!' I gasp a second later, reaching for

a cup of water. The table has six chairs around it, but we're the only two here. The rest of the dining room buzzes with noise and activity, and there's a little quiet space around us. 'Are they really food?'

'They're an acquired taste.' She sniffs, grabbing a handful. 'Anyway, enough about food. You're OK for me to come over later so we can look for the rift?'

'Do you think it's possible?'

'All things are possible,' she says, taking a cheese straw and waving it at me. 'How can you of all people doubt that?'

'Some things can't be changed.'

She gives me a look, and for a second her eyes are full of shadows, but she forces them away with a breath and a toss of her hair. 'And some things do change. Look. Grace is staring at you.'

'So?'

'So a week ago she wouldn't even have known you were here. Stuff changes, Bavar. All the time. It has to.' She breaks the cheese straw in two, hands me half. Her eyes are shining. 'It just has to.'

Aoife is suspicious. She's had us trapped in the kitchen for the last twenty minutes trying out her latest fudge brownies, making us talk about school and homework. To start with, Angel looked happy enough about it, trying to answer all the questions with her mouth full, but now she's looking a bit shifty. Her eyes keep darting to the door, and her feet tap against the wooden rung of the chair like a drumbeat that won't stop until it has all the answers. And Aoife doesn't want to let us go. I don't know how much she heard last night, whether she suspects what we're up to, but I know she won't like it. She says it isn't possible to close the rift. I think she's afraid that it might just make things worse.

Is that possible?

I try to imagine what a rift to another world could possibly look like. The sky glows amber when they attack, and I've always imagined it as a fiery abyss, but it could be anything. What kind of door could hide that sort of thing? I've racked my brain for clues, but I can't find any, and thinking about it just makes me nervous. Sitting by fidgety Angel is making me nervous too.

'Talking of homework,' I say loudly, interrupting them and pushing my chair back with a screech. 'We should make a start.'

Angel nods, grabbing another wedge of brownie as she stands up.

165

'Why don't you do it here?' Aoife asks.

'Oh. Because . . . we're going to use the *Computer*.'

'Ah, the *Computer*.' She nods, and takes a copper pot from one of the hooks over the window. 'Very well. I'll call you when dinner is ready.'

'What's the *Computer*?' Angel hisses as we head for the stairs.

'It's in my mother's room,' I say, ignoring the whisper of the ancestors as we get to the first landing. 'She used it to invite people to the parties. It's probably one of the first computers ever made, but it does have the *Internet* on it, so it's a good excuse. Also, her room is in the old part of the house, and that's a good place to start looking . . .'

Looking looking looking, echoes through the house. Uncle Sal pops out of his study. 'Looking? What for?' He lifts his glasses and rubs at his eyes. 'Ah, Angel – I *thought* they were excited about something . . .' He glowers up at the nearest portrait, of a thin girl with reddish hair and a wicked smile. She arches her curved brows at him, and he turns his back on her with a huff. 'What's going on, Bavar? What are you two looking for?'

'Madness!' bursts Angel. We both stare at her. 'Madness, in *Lord of the Flies*. For English. We're going to use the *Computer*!'

166

Angel

They have a *Computer*! With the *Internet* on it! They all say the words like they're talking about aliens. Sal looks a bit dubious about our homework mission, but I'm not sure he really likes people very much, so after an awkward moment he lifts a hand and darts back into wherever he came from, closing the door firmly.

'So,' I say, turning to Bavar. 'Where shall we start?'

My blood is pumping because we're really *doing* this. I feel light as a bird, full of possibility, and then I look up and he's all shadowy, looming over me like some sort of spectre.

'What's bugging you?' I whisper, trying to hide a shudder.

'Nothing.'

I fold my arms, tapping my foot. He beetles his

eyebrows at me. He has amazing eyebrows, thick and curved.

'Come on, just tell me.'

He sighs, and wanders across the landing to a narrow window that looks across the frost-covered fields. The sun is low in the sky, and shadows stretch across glittering grass.

'I just don't think it's going to be as easy as you think,' he says, his breath huffing out at the glass.

'How hard can it be to find a *door*? There are, like . . . ten in Pete and Mary's house, if you don't count the cupboards!'

'You've seen this place, right?' He spreads his arms.

'Yes, but even so! I mean, what, maybe a hundred doors?'

'But then there are the hidden ones. And what's a door, anyway?'

'What do you mean, "what's a door?" Surely a door is a door? So high –' I reach up – 'so wide . . . Look, there's one right there.' I march over and pat the solid wood of the nearest door. 'For example . . .'

'That's just an *ordinary* door,' he huffs. 'We're not looking for an ordinary door, are we? Who knows what a door to a rift looks like. It might be like . . .

a tree, or a chimney. Anything!'

'So what,' I demand. 'You're not just going to give up already, are you? We haven't even started yet!'

'I'm not going to give up,' he says. 'I'm just warning you, it might take a while. You don't seem like the most patient person in the world, so I thought I'd say.'

'Fine,' I say. 'I am warned, thank you very much. Now, where shall we start?'

'Let's get away from here, anyway,' he mutters. 'Sal will be even worse than Aoife if he realizes what we're up to.'

'Why?' I ask. 'I mean, surely they don't like being plagued by monsters every evening?'

'Raksasa,' he says absently, starting down the corridor. 'And no, they don't like it. But it's all we've done for a long time, so I think they probably just want me to get over it and start fighting them off properly.'

'Killing them?'

He winces. 'Ultimately, yes.'

'I thought I wanted that,' I say. 'When I saw you fighting before, I was kind of egging you on. And then you did kill it.'

'I didn't . . .'

'Well, you know, we *thought* you had. And I realized what it cost you.'

'So you don't want me to kill them?'

'No, not if it hurts you. I want to stop them coming.'

'Well, that's why we're doing this,' he says, gesturing up a narrow wooden staircase.

'Yes. I just . . . I wanted you to know. In case you have any doubts. I don't know what it'll be like, when we find this thing.' I clatter up the steps, his slow footsteps heavier behind me. 'But it'll be fine. It'll be the right thing to do.' I look back at him. 'Whatever happens, Bavar, we'll do it.'

As I say it, I don't know whether I'm trying to reassure myself or him, and either way it sounds a bit hollow. He doesn't reply, and for a split second I am caught in a moment of total unreality, scarpering up narrow steps in a strange house, with an even stranger boy, looking for a window to a monster world. I take a breath and keep going anyway.

One step at a time.

This whole place is so incredible. The further we walk, the more we see, the more I feel in tune with it. Every part of it just gets better, darker, weirder, and there's so *much* of it. There are little sunrooms with balconies, cupboards bigger than my bedroom, sitting rooms full of covered furniture. Cobwebs drape from the ceilings of little box rooms, dust thick on patterned carpets. I go into each one, poke around, open things, prod wood panels and crumbling lintels, and Bavar follows me like a cloud. He watches sceptically as I carry out my checks, and then we're back out into the corridors to face yet more of those portraits with their waxy faces and large, dark eyes watching our every move.

'Who *are* all these people?' I ask eventually.

'Relatives, ancestors,' Bavar says, keeping his head bent. 'Better if you just ignore them, really.'

'Why, what are they going to do?' I ask, stopping. I turn to the nearest, of a young woman, dark hair knotted on top of her head, brown eyes wide and knowing. There's a bit of a sneer on her face. 'I mean, I know they can be a bit loud . . . Ooh, look, this one's called Bloodwyn Victorious. She looks . . . nice . . .'

The constant whispering gets louder, and indistinct words roar around me, like the sea getting rough. Bloodwyn looks me up and down and hisses, revealing pointed grey teeth. I jump back, all the little hairs on my skin standing on end.

'Is that why you put the plants on the graves? So they won't shout at you?'

Bavar pulls me away, pushes me down the corridor. 'You'll get them all going – I told you to ignore them!' His shadow looms over mine, and a shudder rolls down my back

But it's OK. What's the worst that could happen? The worst already happened, I remind myself. This is just a sideshow.

'Where shall we look, then?' I've lost count of the rooms we've checked. It must be dozens, surely, and yet it feels like we've hardly begun. I'm beginning to see Bavar's earlier point. Not that I'm going to tell him that. 'Do you think these guys will help us?' I peer up at the next portrait, a jowly man in a frilly collar called Lionel. 'Hey,' I whisper.

He blinks.

'Do you know where the secret door is? The one that leads to the . . .'

Bavar pushes me on before I can finish.

'They might know!' I protest.

'And then what? They'll tell Aoife . . . and then it'll all be over.'

I look up at him. 'Do you really think she can stop you if you want to do this?'

He blows his cheeks out. 'I don't know. I'd rather

not find out. Let's check up here.'

'Why is it all closed up?' I ask, as he mutters a curse and pulls hard on a heavy wooden door that leads to yet more corridors, all the same wood panelling, and dark maze carpet. We've been up and down and around, and now I've no idea where we are – it wouldn't be a surprise if the next stop was back at the kitchen, to be honest.

'There are only three of us here now,' he says. 'We don't need all these rooms.'

'It feels weird. Like the house doesn't like it.'

'It got used to being busier. Parties, that kind of thing, when my parents were here.' He mooches forward, and lights wink on as he approaches, throwing shadows up on to the patterned wallpaper.

'How do you do that?'

'What?' He turns to me.

'The lights – they come on when you're near!'

'Oh –' he looks up – 'I'm the master of the house.'

I look at him. 'The *Master of the House*?' I intone with a grin.

'I didn't say it like that!'

'Well, still. What does that mean, really?'

'It means I'm connected to it,' he says. 'The magic that opened the rift and brought the raksasa affects everything. Me, the paintings, the lights . . .'

'So your parents were like you, then. And they fought the monsters –' I look up at the portraits – 'and so did all these guys?'

He nods, as a woman lying on a couch bares her teeth at me from the nearest painting.

'So where did they go then, your parents?'

'I don't know,' he says shortly, turning to a new corridor on the right. 'Let's try through here.'

'Why did they go?'

'They made a mistake.'

'And so what, they just ran away, left you here? How could they do that?'

He looks like I slapped him and I curse myself. Mouth before mind – Dad used to tell me that sometimes. 'Think first,' he'd say. 'And if you think you might regret it, perhaps you shouldn't say it.'

'Sorry,' I say. 'I didn't mean . . .'

'Yeah, you did,' he says. 'And yeah, they just ran away and left me here.' His voice shakes, and he wanders off ahead of me, into the shadows. 'So let's just get on with this.'

Bavar

I used to play hide-and-seek in these corridors. My father would chase me, roaring, until I darted off, and then I'd scrabble for the right place, and he'd stalk the carpeted floors, hollering at every doorway. It was our favourite game, though I'm not sure it was really a fair one. The winner was usually whoever managed to get the ancestors on their side, and because I was smaller and less forbidding, it was usually me. They'd all start shouting, sending echoes through the house to confuse him, giving him false starts and misinformation until he headed off in the wrong direction, while I pressed myself in tight behind a curtain, or crouched behind a chest. It would always take him ages to find me. When I was looking though, that was different. They'd spy on him for me and show me the way, whispering me along to wherever he was hiding. He always acted like he was cross about it, crying out at them, calling them traitors and threatening to hold a bonfire with their portraits. But I knew he wasn't angry really – it was all just part of the game.

Now that I think about it, I wonder how I never knew there was a door with a rift behind it. Surely I'd have noticed. Or at least he'd have stopped me getting anywhere near it. But the house is funny like that; it stretches and contracts, and even familiar passageways seem to take on new twists and turns, depending on the time of day, or the mood you're in. And I haven't been up here for a long time. The corridors are dark and ghostly with white sheets. Aoife has shut off entire parts of the house because we don't need them. We used to need them, when my parents held their parties. There were always people here. And then the mistake happened: they had neglected the barrier, one of the raksasa escaped, and then they fled, leaving me with Aoife and Sal, and overnight everything changed.

'It's *so* creepy,' breathes Angel now, as we step into another dark, empty room, the windows obscured by wooden shutters, cobwebs trailing from the door frame. Has there ever, in the history of this house, been anyone like this here? She's so determined. She can't possibly understand what all this means, and yet she seems so sure. She darts ahead of me like a small, bright moth, examining every dark corner, fingering every wall hanging as though she might find the answers there, while I just flounder along behind her, fighting with all my doubts.

It could be the biggest mistake of all time, letting her in on it all like this. The figures in the portraits are very dubious about the whole thing, up here. They've been in the shadows for so long, they're startled, their eyes blinking, as if someone just opened the curtains and they're being blinded by the sun.

Or by a girl, whose name just happens to be Angel.

She stops at a ceiling-high, ornately carved wooden door at the end of a wide, carpeted corridor, and glances back at me.

'What do you think? Will this be the one?' she asks, for what feels like the hundredth time.

'Shouldn't think so,' I say, reaching out and twisting the handle. My hand is shaking. I clutch harder, feeling her sharp eyes on me, and honestly I almost hope it is the flipping rift, right now. Maybe I could just disappear into it and get a little peace and quiet.

*

It's the ballroom, which isn't exactly what I'd planned on. I'm a little bit disorientated now, and starting to wonder if the house is playing tricks on us. This room has so many memories, I was hoping to avoid it altogether, and I know it's not the right place for the door; it's too public for a secret doorway. Angel looks around, her eyes sparkling. At least being in here will distract her for a bit, before she pulls me apart again with all her clever thoughts and words. They sting. Like everyone talked to me through cotton wool before, and she's taken it off and thrown it away, making everything clear.

I haven't been in here for years. The crystal chandeliers are rimed in cobwebs now, pale sheets covering the grand piano, and a dozen tables and chairs scattered through the room. The floor is black marble, but there's a grey carpet of dust that softens our footsteps. Ghosts of the past flicker in the corners of my eyes: I see my father leading my mother in a waltz, the room captivated by their superhuman elegance; butlers staggering under trays laden with glasses and bottles; guests in ornate masks, laughing.

'Bavar!' The voice of an elderly woman cuts through

the memories. 'Look how you've grown!' The steely eyes of Great-aunt Rebecca look me up and down from the ornate brass frame on the picture rail. Angel looks up. 'My, and it seemed just yesterday . . . but who is this? You have a friend with you?'

'It's Angel.'

'Of course it is,' Rebecca says. 'I heard the mutterings, though we never see anything these days. That Aoife –' she shakes her head, her eyes narrowed – 'such a spoilsport. Always was, even when she was a child. No interest in the magic, just wanted her books, and her little tea parties with her dollies . . .'

I blink, trying to imagine it. A small dark-haired girl, serious amidst all the madness of this place. I wonder what my mother was like then. Were they ever close? I know they couldn't stand each other, when Aoife came back with Sal.

'Come then, Angel,' Rebecca says briskly. 'Let me see you . . . give me a twirl. Now aren't you sweet! Wonderful, even in these modern clothes of yours. A nice brocade dress, and you'd just about sparkle. Oh, you should have seen the parties, the people! So beautiful, oh yes, they knew how to dress for the occasion in those days . . . !'

'We should go,' I say, seeing Angel's eyes glint dangerously at the idea of a brocade dress. 'Got things to do . . .'

'Yes,' Rebecca says, her eyes sharp. 'Looking for things, eh? Well, I'll let you get on. Go careful, the both of you . . . Oh, Bavar!'

'Yes?' I ask, turning back.

'How's my grave? Are you keeping it nice, down there? These things matter, you know.'

'He's looking after it all,' Angel says. 'Lovely flowers, all sorts . . .'

Rebecca nods, apparently satisfied. 'Jasmine, I think? Sometimes I can smell it, when the wind blows the right way. Didn't I say so, Rupert?' She raises her voice. 'JASMINE.'

'Oh, I like jasmine,' says my great-uncle, from the next portrait, looking up. 'Always liked jasmine. Good to have, when you're keeping watch at night. Soothing, I always thought . . .'

I nod at him and bare my teeth at both of them in a sort-of smile before hurrying Angel away.

'Why did you do that?' she demands, looking back at them. 'They were still talking!'

'If we stop to hear all their stories, we'll never get

180

anywhere,' I tell her. I don't tell her that they remind me of other times, when my parents were here, and of how things have changed, how lonely it all seems in this place now. 'We should keep going; it won't be long before Aoife starts looking for us.'

'OK,' she says, breaking away from me and running to the ornate fireplace at the end of the room and inspecting it closely, pressing at the flowers carved into the pale marble.

'What are you doing?'

'Maybe this is the door . . . maybe if we find the right button . . .'

'They're not buttons; they're flowers!'

She ignores me and runs her fingers over the mantelpiece, standing on tiptoes to reach it.

'Angel . . .'

'Ah!' she exclaims, turning to me with a smile, pulling on something just beneath the ledge. 'Found something!' The fireplace shudders, and there's a violent grinding sound as it begins to swing around. 'I knew it!' she grins, as a dark void opens up where the fireplace stood, dust and old plaster raining down around us. 'I *knew* it would be a fireplace!'

I pull her back, my chest thudding, and I realize

181

I still haven't thought this through properly. I didn't think we'd really find it. What if there's suddenly a great void to a monstrous alternate universe? What if we get sucked in?

'Oh,' Angel says, peeking around me. 'That doesn't look right . . .'

Angel

'It's Uncle Sal's office!' Bavar turns to me, panicking. 'Quick, get back – how do we close this?' He looks around desperately.

I'm a bit gutted to be honest. I was imagining some fiery hellhole, not more paisley carpet and an old wood desk.

'Angel, where's the lever?' He starts flapping about between the rooms, looking for the marble ledge that swung back into the darkness, his hair sparking with static.

'Calm down!' I say, peering through the gap to the study. 'He's not even in there.'

'He might come back any minute!'

'So what?' I demand.

'He'll be furious; there'll be all sorts of shouting. I

don't know what he does in here, but whatever it is he won't want us poking around!'

'But we found a secret doorway, Bavar! We found a revolving fireplace! I mean, you didn't know this was here, did you?'

'No . . .'

'So stop worrying and let's do this! Who knows where it might lead us.' I squeeze past him, ducking down until I'm into the study. Rows of shelves stretch to the ceiling, full of books, and between them sit smoky old snow globes and strange copper gadgets that wink in the light of an angular lamp. The desk is overflowing with old ledgers and papers full of spidery handwriting. 'I mean, I don't know, you could spy on him!'

'I think that would probably just be really boring,' Bavar says, scrunching down low before emerging next to me. 'He's writes academic papers about stuff, I don't know, I never really listened . . . We really should get out of here before he comes back . . .'

'But some of the stuff in here is really interesting. Look, here's some kind of compass thing.' I peer down at the round copper paperweight balanced on a stack of tightly written sheets. There's a round green gem glittering in the middle. 'Ooh, look!'

'Don't press it!' Bavar slaps at my hand, but it's too late – the copper thing pops open with a noise like a banshee scream. I clap my hands to my ears, and Bavar picks it up, poking and prodding at it.

'Make it stop!' I shout.

He gives me a murderous look and claps the thing between his hands. The awful noise stops. After a moment he opens his hands warily, and a bunch of tiny golden springs fly out, ricocheting around the room.

'Oh my goodness,' he says. 'We broke it.'

'*You* broke it!' I giggle.

'I don't know why you have to press *every* button you see,' he says, but his mouth twitches, and I'm pretty sure he's trying not to laugh.

'That's the whole point of exploring,' I say. 'Finding stuff, pressing it, finding more stuff, dodging flying springs . . . What is that thing, anyway?'

'Some kind of personal alarm—' He breaks off, tilting his head. 'Quick!' he hisses, balancing the copper thing back on the pile of papers. 'I can hear footsteps!'

'I can't!' I protest, as he drags me back through the gap between rooms. 'Bavar, wait – what about all the little springs?'

'Too late for that! Where's the catch?' He starts

fumbling around. 'Angel – where is it? How do we close this thing?'

'It's just there.' I step forward, gesturing to the mantelpiece, now hidden by the shadows.

He reaches out, but it was a bit fiddly even for me, and I realize his hands are far too big – he'll never manage it. I step in, pulling at the little lever, and we jump out of the way as the fireplace begins to swing around again. The noise is fairly impressive, but finally the whole thing settles and the ballroom looks pretty much like it did before.

'Well, that was exciting!' I say.

Bavar stares at me.

'He's going to know we were there. We broke the alarm. He'll find all those springs on the carpet.'

'I'm not sure about that; it's pretty chaotic in there,' I say. 'And I'm not sure the alarm was working properly anyway – was it meant to scream like that?'

'Probably not,' he concedes.

'Can't do much about it now, anyway. Unless you want to go back and tell him what happened?' I gesture at the fireplace. 'I mean, it might be worth it for the look on his face when we burst through the chimney!'

His mouth twitches again.

'He'd be cross.'

'I don't know why you're scared of him – he's about the size of your knee!'

The words come out a bit high because I'm trying not to laugh, and then they echo around the room unnaturally and I realize the people in the portraits are repeating me, their shoulders shuddering with laughter. Bavar stares around at them, and then looks down at me.

'What have you done to this place?' he asks. His eyes are brighter than I've ever seen them, and I realize that maybe, just maybe, he's even beginning to enjoy this, just a little bit, in spite of all his panicking.

'Livened it up a bit.' I grin. 'That's all. You shouldn't worry so much. Didn't you ever do anything naughty before?'

'Not really,' he says.

'Why?'

He shrugs. I stare at him.

'Just didn't,' he says. 'There wasn't anyone here to be naughty with. And my parents were pretty fierce.'

'Oh.' I swallow. I wonder what it was like, and imagine two grown-up Bavars, both as brooding as he is. It must've been pretty intense.

'Oh, stop looking like that,' he says. 'They were fine, just . . .'

'A bit intense,' I say, nodding. I look at him and grin. 'I think I get it.'

'Ha ha,' he says drily. 'Come on then.' He pulls me forward. 'Let's see what else we can find to liven things up. Only you're *not* to press any more buttons.'

The laughter bursts out – I can't help it. The sight of him flapping about with that alarm and all the springs pinging up at him, the look of surprise on his face. Brilliant. He's just brilliant.

Bavar

My heart is jumping at the thought of actually finding the rift and being able to do something about it. I guess I never thought it would actually happen. I didn't think any of this was possible. I thought I'd just be here forever, shoring up the barrier. But we already found one secret doorway, and who knows how many more there will be. Every corridor, every nook and cranny suddenly seems full of possibility. Angel's conviction is so powerful, I can't help getting carried along by it. I pull her up another narrow little staircase, concentrating on not banging my head, and by the time we reach the next corridor we're both covered in dust, looking a bit like ghosts ourselves.

'I'm sure I've just eaten a spider.' She grimaces, swiping cobwebs from her sleeves and bunching her shoulders up around her neck with a shudder.

'I didn't think you'd worry about a little thing like a spider,' I say.

'I don't like them.'

'You're OK with the raksasa though . . .'

'Well, they're not so fiddly. They won't get into your ears or down your top.' She shudders. 'Ugh.'

We check the little dark rooms off the corridor, old servants' bedrooms with narrow wardrobes, all of which Angel insists upon checking, as though we're looking for Narnia, and then the way opens out into the main house again, and we get to the wing I shared with my parents, before they went.

The rooms here are bigger, the ceilings higher, and somehow it's all just a bit grander. Oversized furniture looms up over us, and ornate chandeliers tinkle as we pass, sending yet more dust to cover us.

Aoife never liked it in this part of the house. Even when Mother and Father were here, she said it didn't feel like a home, more like a museum. When they left she moved us all to the south wing, where the main kitchen is and the light streams brighter through the windows. I didn't mind; I was happy to have a new start. The rooms fit better. It felt cosy. Homely, I guess.

190

Being back here now is unnerving; familiar, and yet different. The air is cold and stale, and the portraits in the corridors watch with haughty gazes, as if they're offended by our presence.

'Ooh, look at this!' Angel calls from the room ahead.

I hurry after her. It doesn't sound like an 'I've found the portal' sort of voice, but I'm learning you can never tell with her.

'It's beautiful!' She turns to me with a look of wonder on her face as I walk in, and I can't help but smile. It's the orangery that sits at the top of one of the towers. Of course. How is it that I've become such a stranger in my own home? How could I forget about this place? A stained-glass dome rises up above us, tiny intricate panels of blue and green leading up to a rose in the centre.

'Don't you ever come in here?' she asks in a hushed voice.

'No,' I say, looking up, watching the light change as the clouds shift. It's dusk, and that eerie grey light makes the whole room seem to glow, colours dancing in the dust on the floor. All around the edges of the room are enormous terracotta pots, and the trees within are spindly and grey-tinged with neglect. There are green leaves among the pale, dry ones, new shoots still shining with life.

'It seems a shame,' Angel says, turning and turning. 'What did you do in here?'

I shrug, but the picture is already there in my mind. This was where Mother would come on quiet days, where she'd read, or try to do embroidery. I don't think she was very good at it; I never found a finished one. The trees were thriving then, glossy green leaves and tiny orange fruits that she would share with me.

Angel is like a kid in a toy shop. She starts uncovering elegant, high-backed sofas and little wooden tables, and then she finds matches in a box on an old mahogany dresser, and lights the candles in the brass sconces that line the walls.

'It's amazing,' she says, as the room takes on a new, warmer glow. She pulls at another of the cloths to reveal a small piano, where my father would sit and play. I flinch when it emerges. It was the most at rest I ever saw him, caught up in the music. I can almost hear it still . . . almost see him sitting there, his tall, narrow frame curved over as he played.

'Can you play?' Angel asks, rolling back the dark wood cover to reveal the keys. She fingers them gently,

192

and the notes are a mellow whisper that make my chest ache.

'Used to, a bit,' I say.

'Show me?'

I look around. It's a quiet room; it always was. No portraits in here, just small paintings of landscapes: moonlight on a lake; the house under the amber glow of what a stranger might think was only the sunset; tiny songbirds on silver branches.

'I don't know what to play.' The piano seems so small; the stool is like a perch. I sit there, and she beams at me, and so I feel like I should try. But my mind is blank.

Sometimes, when you're not thinking, your body seems to know just what it's doing all by itself. My fingers are clumsy at first, about four times too big for the keys, all knuckles and far too heavy. How did Father do it? I close my eyes, flinching on the inside, remembering what it was like in those rare moments when they were both here and we pretended that was all that ever existed.

'Softer, Bavar – let it come out of you. You don't have to push so hard . . .' My father's voice, almost a whisper.

193

I don't know what the piece of music is called, but I remember how it filled the room, rose up to the peak of the dome and seemed to settle there, ringing long after the last note was played. How we'd sit, and my mother would tell stories while the stars came out.

There *were* good times here. I'd almost forgotten.

Angel

Wow.

I never saw anyone play the piano like that.

I don't know whether it's the magic in the house, or the memories of this room, or just Bavar, but the whole place comes alive with it, and outside it gets darker, but in here there's a hazy golden glow, as candlelight plays with dust motes that dance in the music. The leaves in the dome glitter, the glass rose blooms, and the birds in the pictures shuffle their wings, turning their bright eyes to watch him.

He's so lost to it. His fingers move faster and faster, his whole body seems just an extension of the piano, and he's not scrunching himself up, or trying to hide, he's not moping or glowering or waiting for bad things to happen – he's just there, playing like it's the only thing in the world . . . and so it is, for a while.

The last note rings out for a long time after he finishes. I watch as all the things come back in to bother him, as his eyes flick to the sky outside, watching for danger, and then to the door, and finally to me.

'The rift!' he says. 'We keep getting distracted.'

'Yeah,' I say, giving myself a little shake. 'Let's find the rift.' I trace a pattern on the dusty wooden floor with my toe as he goes around blowing out candles, and a fine line appears beneath my feet, crossing the floorboards.

'Hey, look!' I whisper, bending and uncovering more of the line. 'It's a trapdoor!'

'It's not a trapdoor.' He kneels next to me. 'I never noticed a trapdoor in here!'

'Maybe there was a rug over it before,' I say.

'It's probably just a fault in the wood.'

'How do we open it?' I ask.

'It can't be a trapdoor,' he protests, poking around anyway, looking for an opening.

I shove the table back to get more space, and as I shove it, the floor he's inspecting begins to rise. He jumps back with a shout, and I can't help but grin.

196

'Behold the trapdoor,' I say grandly, with a bit of a bow.

'Well, but it's not the rift,' he says, bending and looking into the darkness. 'It looks like the pantry to me!'

'What?' I dart forward, and peer into a small, dark room, a chink of light along one side revealing shelf after shelf of bottles and tins and jars, industrial-sized bags of tea and sugar, and great sacks of potatoes on a rough stone floor. 'Why would anyone have a trapdoor to a *food cupboard*?'

I look up at him, outraged.

'I guess it's as good a place as any to hide, if there was an emergency,' he says, his eyes sparkling. 'Plenty of food and nobody'd know you were there.'

'Who needs that many potatoes, anyway? There's only three of you.'

We peer down for a while. My stomach rumbles treacherously; it's been a long time since lunch.

'Come on,' he says, finally, sounding a bit reluctant. 'We'd better just close it, before Aoife finds us.'

'But I'm hungry – let's do some foraging!' I scramble over the edge, dropping down into the pantry. It's a longer drop than I thought it'd be, to be honest, and the stone floor is a hard landing. 'Oof!'

'Angel!' he hisses, reaching down. 'Get out of there!'

'It's incredible!' I whisper. Like being in a treasure cave, only instead of gold and jewels, it's full, ram-packed with every kind of food. Shiny foil packages, paper bags with tiny labels, bottles that wink in the light. I realize I don't actually recognize most of it. I've no clue what semolina is, and desiccated coconut sounds pretty awful. There are various sorts of mouldy-looking sausage stacked in one corner, and right in front of me the most enormous tin of black treacle, oozing darkness – I guess that's a favourite in Aoife's cooking.

Bavar is still hissing at me overhead. I tune him out and keep scanning; surely there'll be biscuits here somewhere. But before I can find them, there's a mumbling noise from the other side of the pantry door. The latch starts to lift. I grab it, stopping it getting any further and hushing up at Bavar, who looks like he's about to explode.

'Onions, onions,' comes Aoife's voice. 'Oh, this blessed door!' There's a thump against the wood, as if she's kicking at it. I realize I'm trapped; I can't let go of the latch or she'll catch me here.

I look up at Bavar with a grimace. He disappears.

Well.

That's less than helpful.

What am I going to do now?

'AOIFE!' comes a great roar through the house.

The latch stops wiggling.

'What's he roaring about?' comes her muffled voice, footsteps heading away from the pantry.

'Come on,' pants Bavar, appearing again at the trapdoor. 'Quickly! She's on her way now – nobody else is allowed in her pantry!'

'Well, you roared at her,' I say, grabbing at a bag of something as I climb up the shelves and let him pull me out. 'So of course she's coming.'

'What did you want me to do?'

'I don't know. I think I'd have thought of something better than that.'

He pulls a face as I scramble up, and shoves the table back, watching closely as the trapdoor closes. 'Well, I wanted to make sure. I don't want her to know about this; it might be useful, for midnight snacking purposes . . .' He looks down at the bag I grabbed on my way up. 'I mean, who doesn't need instant access to dried mushrooms?'

Now he's laughing.

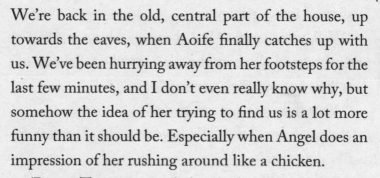

Bavar

We're back in the old, central part of the house, up towards the eaves, when Aoife finally catches up with us. We've been hurrying away from her footsteps for the last few minutes, and I don't even really know why, but somehow the idea of her trying to find us is a lot more funny than it should be. Especially when Angel does an impression of her rushing around like a chicken.

'Bavar! There you are!' she clucks, when she finally runs into us, wiping her hands on a floral apron, looking for all the world like a flustered hen. 'What was all that shouting about?'

'Oh, we were just having a look around, and I wanted to show her how the sound travels . . .' My voice trails off and I look at Angel desperately, trying to keep my face serious.

'How sound travels?' Aoife demands, looking between us with bright eyes. 'I thought there was an emergency!'

'It was my fault,' says Angel, clearing her throat and refusing to look at me. 'I challenged him. Didn't think anyone would hear us from so far away! He was just giving me a tour, really – being polite . . . And anyway, he says this is the old bit, the original house, and everything else came after . . . It's all *so* fascinating.'

Aoife narrows her eyes. 'I'm making dinner,' she says, looking us both up and down. 'Ten minutes.'

'OK,' I say, shifting back up against the wall.

'Way to look suspicious, Bavar!' Angel whispers as Aoife makes her way down the stairs with a backward glance.

'What do you mean?'

'Did you never have to lie before?'

'Uh . . . no.'

'Well, it shows. You should practise.'

'It was all your "fascinating" rubbish that got her suspicious!' I protest.

'Ah, whatever,' she says. 'Quick, let's try in here first, before dinner.' She gestures at the next door and marches to it, shooting me a look. 'What's dinner going to be exactly?'

'I don't know. Probably some kind of meat.' I sigh and follow her, ignoring a little portrait of my mother up high on the wall between a couple of mirrors and an old sketch of the town, hoping it's going to stay silent. I couldn't bear to hear her voice right now. Couldn't bear the look on Angel's face if she realized who it was. I don't know what she'd make of her, but I know she'd be curious, and there would be questions, and I've had about enough of all that today. 'Aoife likes meat.'

'Bet it'll have onions,' Angel says. 'Onion gravy, maybe . . .' She looks up at me, all bright-eyed, but I don't reply, because she's standing right in front of a door that shouldn't be here. There are hundreds of doors in this house, and dozens I've seen today that I can't say I really remembered very clearly. But this one . . . this one rings with wrongness. It's taller, narrower than the rest, the wood is a reddish-brown, and it looks brittle and dry, like an old dying tree.

'Well anyway, it'll probably be better than Mary's fish pie,' Angel says, pulling on the pitted, tarnished handle. She wiggles it and pushes, and then shoves at the wood with her shoulder, but it won't budge.

'Who's Mary?' I ask, a bit distracted, reaching out to the door, my mother's eyes following me.

'My foster mother,' she says, still straining at the wood. Her tone is neutral, careless. But when I look down, her shoulders are high, tensed up around her neck, and I know that feeling.

'Why do you have a foster mother?'

'My parents died,' she says. 'I told you the other night; you were a bit out of it. Come on, let's do this.' She gestures at the door, moving away to let me get closer. 'Open it already!'

'But . . .'

This is a bad idea.

'Bavar, just do it! We can talk about stuff later; I want to know what's here!'

'BAVAR!' comes Aoife's voice. And Angel glowers at me and I could just keep going with this door but I already know it's going to change everything, and I'm not sure I'm ready for that.

Her parents died.

I wish I could remember what she told me. I want to know if it's connected. I want to ask how they died. But I can't because there's an ache at the base of my stomach when she looks at me, and I don't want to go there.

Not yet.

'Come on,' I say, turning my back on it all. 'We'll come back to it.'

'No!'

'Uh – yes!' I charge out on to the main landing. After a moment she catches up with me, her arms folded. 'I promise, we'll find it straight after dinner.'

'Yes, *Master*,' she says eventually in a little voice. 'I know we will.'

I look back at her.

'Seriously?'

'Seriously, *Master*,' she says with a cunning smile. 'Look, I've left some clues – just in case you *forget* which way it was.'

I look back, and see that she really has. Not exactly breadcrumbs, but bits of her stuff, in a trail. A pen, some keys, a few books. They look like little islands in a vast sea, just pulling us back to that door. I shudder, and start down the stairs at a run.

Angel

There was a kind of pie, with various colours of mash, and we ate off platters with long, thin knives and forks that weighed a tonne. And Aoife and Sal talked about how the potatoes weren't doing so well this year, their eyes constantly flicking from me to Bavar. And he just lowered his head and ate a mountain of food, and then there was tea, and cake. I swear, I wouldn't at this point be surprised if the whole house was actually made of cake.

I look at one of the walls and narrow my eyes, and then laugh at myself. If it was made of cake, it'd be a lot prettier, anyway. It's all so dark. Dark paint, only broken by darker wallpaper. The floors are polished black wood, and the rugs are like pathways through bewitched forests, vines and flowers leading you onward, onward, to where I hope at some point I might find a loo.

The ancestors are quiet up on the walls, but their eyes follow me, and Aoife said something about straight on and to the left, or the right, I don't know, I wasn't really listening. I stand there for a moment, a little bit lost, and in the silence something calls to me. A whisper – not in the air but in my blood. Something deep inside, like an itch I can't reach. I step forward, to where the feeling is louder, and it peaks when I get to the ornate door on the right of the great hallway. It's closed, it's always been closed, and I shouldn't go in, I know I shouldn't, but something in there is calling like a heartbeat, like a storm on the inside. I open the door and dart in, pulling it closed behind me.

It's bleak and bare in here, tattered velvet curtains parted at the vast bay window, and an old chaise longue along one wall, faded blue and gold. Over the fireplace is an enormous mirror with a gilded, blackened frame and that . . . that is the thing that calls to me.

I can hear my dad.

I tread lightly over the dusty rug and I keep my head down, and I can barely breathe because I don't want to make a sound. I don't know how, but I can hear his voice and I have this hope, this wild hope that somehow he's going to be here. That when I look up there he'll be, in the mirror, in the room, breathing, talking, living.

I look up. Me, but not me. My hair glows, my eyes are the blue of a bright winter sky, and there, just over my shoulders, sweeping up to the ceiling, a pair of gleaming cloud-pale wings. I blink, and the image is gone.

Hah!

I scowl at my reflection. Pale, scrawny old me, just kidding herself. And then the mirror clouds over. For a moment I can't see anything at all, and then slowly, as I watch, a new scene unfolds behind me. The room isn't a cold, silent place. It's ringing with noise and light, and laughter. Men and women gather in clusters, and in the middle of it all is a couple who shine even brighter than all the rest. They're both tall, and the man has Bavar's hair, though he's tried to tame it and it shines beneath the swinging crystal chandelier. The woman has magic in every movement: when she laughs the whole room brightens, and when she stops there's a sigh, as if the world is trying to hold on to the sound. She looks up at him and those eyes . . . it's Bavar's parents, it must be. I turn to the room, ice down my spine, but there's nothing there, and when I turn back the scene has faded. I look harder, desperate to see more, and another scene appears before me, like the first, except the air is darker, thicker, the room hums with tension. Bavar's parents stand together, their heads bent.

'What does he want, Faolan?' she whispers. Her face is pale, though she still smiles.

Faolan bends to her. 'He says he's found a way . . . I don't know! The man's raving. They've let him in and now he won't go away, and he won't stop speaking of the raksasa!'

'I must *speak* to you!'

A man breaks through the crowd and stands before them. He looks so small, so pale and scared. The whole room stops to watch.

My dad.

His hair is plastered to his head, his coat dripping with rain. His eyes are haunted. I never saw him like this. I never knew he could look like this.

'Look, it's all very well,' Bavar's mother says in a soothing voice, gesturing the musicians to start up again with one hand, smiling brightly as her guests begin to talk once more. 'And we're so pleased to have you drop by, but dear man, this is a party! Let go of these worries of yours, and have a drink.' She grabs a tall, fizzing glass from a waiter's gleaming tray and passes it to him. 'Have some of this.'

'But the monsters, the raksasa . . .'

'Hush now,' she says, putting out one elegant hand to fend it all away. 'What do you know of monsters? It isn't Halloween, is it?' She laughs, but it's a brittle thing and the sound does not carry. 'Come. Faolan, the poor man is half-dead with the cold and the rain, give him something to eat!'

'No, you must listen! They'll come, thicker and faster, the longer the way is open. I've seen it, in other places, and so I knew, when I saw that amber sky . . .' He holds up an old book. 'I found a way – please, I have brought this . . .'

She flinches away from him, and Faolan steps forward and puts his arm around my father, leading him towards a table filled with silver dishes of every kind of food: pastries and tarts, quiches and salads and cheeses and biscuits, jellies and figs and chocolates, Turkish delight and roasted chestnuts. Dad shakes his head, and Faolan passes him a plate, and then the mirror darkens, and the world spins.

'Angel!' Bavar bursts in. 'Why are you in here?'

'Bring him back.' I turn to him. 'Bring him *back*! Make them listen!'

'What did you see?'

'My father – and your parents, turning him away! Make it come back, Bavar. Make them come back!' I stamp my foot. I have never needed anything more. I feel like someone just took all the oxygen out of the air.

He comes towards me, his dark eyes glittering. 'It's just a memory. The mirror holds them. I can't bring them back. It doesn't work like that.'

'How *does* it work?' I look back, reach up and touch the glass. My face looks back at me, all shadow and light. 'Bavar, how do I make it work?'

'I don't know,' he says, looming up behind me, his face distorted in the glass. 'It throws things up; I've never been able to control it . . .'

'I need to see him. Make it come back!'

'I can't!'

'It's important, Bavar. He had a book. He wanted to tell them . . . I think he wanted to tell them how to close the rift!'

'How would he have known anything about it? The mirror plays tricks, Angel. Sometimes I think it just shows you what you want to see!'

'I didn't want to see him like that, all scared. It happened, Bavar, and your parents just fobbed him off with a drink! They were worried about their guests; they didn't want to know!' His face tightens and I can see it's hit a nerve. 'Is that what they were like? Did they care at all about the world they were supposed to be protecting?'

'They spent their *lives* fighting them back,' he says. 'They fought until it was all they were; the fight, and the glory. And you walk in here, and in five minutes you think you've got it all worked out.' He shakes his head, his shoulders tight. 'You should go.'

'I'm not going anywhere.'

We stare at each other for a long time; truthfully I don't know what I'm doing now. Do I really want to stay here, in this place that turned my father away?

You were going to find the rift, and close it.

But if nobody else has, for all this time . . . if they didn't even have the courage to look, then how can we make it work? Maybe it would be a disaster. Maybe we'd just let more of those monsters loose on the world.

'I saw him. He was here,' I say. Bavar looks from me to the mirror, and back again. Dust swirls in the air around us, and it feels like we're trapped in a moment neither one of us ever wanted. What do we do now?

'OK,' he says in a low rumble, eventually.

'You believe me?'

He nods. 'I don't know what it means, though. I never knew . . .' He swallows hard, looks at the floor. 'I didn't know.'

'What shall we do?' I ask, hoping against hope that he might just have the answer, this one time, because my head hurts and my heart hurts even more.

'We should do it,' he says, squaring his shoulders. A flicker of doubt in his eyes. 'Let's just do it. We can't change what already happened . . .'

'. . . but we can do this?' I say, when he runs out of steam.

'We can try.'

He smiles. It's not a particularly happy sort of smile, but there it is, on his face, and I'll take it. It's good enough, for now. I make my own to join it.

Bavar

Her father was here.

She's all pale and quiet, and right now I'd do just about anything to bring her back to life again, so I charge forward, up the stairs, past all the silent, watching ancestors, and she trails after me. My heart is hammering as I get closer to the strange door we found earlier. The little trail she left is like bits of her happiness, all cast aside as if it didn't matter at all.

It matters. It all matters, and it all fits together, and it's like an answer to a question I never knew I had. It's like a chance to end all this and start again.

I've never been so afraid.

A wave of revulsion goes through me as I step up to the door, and I'm sure there's movement between the wood panels, shadows and light flickering past. I jerk back, a cold sweat running between my shoulder blades.

'Just do it,' says Angel, brushing up next to me and leaning hard against the door. 'Come on, before Aoife comes back . . .'

I can hardly breathe though. Deep inside me something just knows this is where it is, this is where all our troubles come from, and I shouldn't disturb it, and I definitely shouldn't do it with Angel standing right next to me like this. But she's so desperate, her face is set with so much pent-up rage, that I can't tell her no. I shove up against the rough wood with my shoulder as she pounds on it with her fists, and there's a wrenching sound as the catch finally surrenders. I hear my mother's voice shouting from the portrait on the wall as the door bursts open, and another world opens up before our eyes, a screaming vortex that reaches out and clutches at us, threatening to pull us in.

Angel

The woman's voice gets louder, more shrill, but it's hard to hear over the roar of the world before us. We should be doing something, this isn't safe. We should step back, get away, because it's going to devour us, it's going to take us and never let us go, but it's mesmerizing, far too beautiful to look away from. A red sky that you could reach out and touch, bursts of orange and yellow spiralling and flaring out towards us. Black figures wheel high above and down below, rivers of gold curl around dark mountains.

'BAVAR!'

The voice is a roar, it makes me start, and suddenly some part of me is howling and desperate to get away from this before it's too late. I grab Bavar's arm and pull at him, but he's watching like he'll never stop, his whole body turned to the burning sky.

'Bavar, come away!'

'Look at it,' he breathes. 'Can you feel it, Angel?' His eyes gleam as he pulls away from my grip. 'I never knew it could feel like that . . .'

'BAVAR!'

That same woman's voice, darker now, stronger, it reaches out and curls around us, makes him flinch. His mother's voice – I recognize it from the scene in the mirror – though it sounds darker now, amplified by the power in the air.

'COME AWAY FROM THE RIFT, BAVAR.'

'It's not like I thought,' he whispers, stepping closer. His face glows with the light, and the sense of magic around him that normally feels like static is rolling off him, full and easy, like sunlight.

'CLOSE THE DOOR,' the voice says. 'MY BOY, YOU AREN'T READY FOR THIS!'

'What do you care?' he shouts, still fixated on the rift. The swooping creatures in the flare-lit sky are getting closer now, and the air around Bavar warps, hot and heavy. Somehow he's pulling power from the rift. What if he stumbles and falls in? I reach out, wincing, and it stings but I pull at him anyway, and he resists me, takes another step towards the world of the raksasa.

'BAVAR! I ALWAYS CARED . . . EVEN WHEN YOU COULD NOT SEE IT!' The woman's voice rises in desperation. 'PLEASE, COME AWAY NOW.'

He doesn't even hear her. Trails of gold sparkle in the orange sky before us as the raksasa rise and fall on a hot wind, twisting and calling to each other. Beneath the wings, their bodies are almost human in shape, and there's a joy in their movements that even I can see. They call to each other, and their voices make the air ring. He's dazzled by it. What *would* happen if he went in? Is that what he's thinking? That he'd just grow wings and fly, free of care?

'Bavar!' I pull again, harder. What if I lost him here? If I lost him, and I just had to go home, to the little house and Mary and Pete, and the jumpers, and all the not fitting, and missing the people I'll never see again.

'NO! I need you here!' I haul at him, closing my eyes and gritting my teeth, absolutely never, never letting go, no matter what, even if he pulls me in there with him, I'm not giving up. 'BAVAR!' Something lends me strength in that moment, and as I pull he falters, stumbling back, away from the call of the raksasa.

'Close the door,' I say, breathing hard.

He stares down at my hand, still clutching his sleeve. 'You have to close it.'

'But we found it,' he says, turning back to it. 'The rift! It's right here!'

'Yes, but . . .'

I'm so tired. The air burns, my eyes are streaming, and he wants this so desperately. The sense of it all seems to wither as the world before us darkens to nightfall, a scatter of stars and a strange blue moon appearing in the sky. I can't make him do anything. He takes another step back towards the rift.

'YOU NEED THE SPELL!' the woman's voice says. 'YOU CANNOT WIN THIS BATTLE WITHOUT WEAPONS!'

He's standing there, just gazing into the rift.

'CATALYST,' comes the voice now, like cool water against my mind, so sure of itself. 'BRING HIM BACK. YOU CAN DO THIS. DO IT, OR WE ARE ALL LOST . . .'

A great roar goes through the house, and it throws me into action. I brace myself, stretching out, pulling him back and hauling on the door until it bangs shut, the sound echoing all around us.

*

218

'What on earth is going on?' shouts Aoife, running at us as we slide down the wall opposite the door, both of us exhausted and battered with heat and smoke. 'What was that?' She looks from us up to the little portrait high up on the wall. 'What did you do?' she demands.

The dark-haired woman in the portrait says nothing, her eyes are on Bavar, who stares back at her.

'Come!' Aoife snaps. 'Away from here, both of you! I don't know what this is, but you look like you barely survived it!'

Bavar

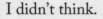

I didn't think.

I wasn't thinking. I was just looking, feeling the power in the rift as it glowed before me, a living, breathing thing that wanted me, that craved me and soothed me and called to me in a million bright voices. I could feel it in my blood, in my heartbeat. I could have dived in, I wanted to, and then my mother's voice was there. I didn't want to hear it. I didn't want to leave, to stop feeling that power. And then it was Angel, and I couldn't hide it from her. I couldn't leave her.

'How did you close the door?' I ask, as we traipse after Aoife. She's absolutely furious, striding along, the lights flickering in her wake, the ancestors all struck dumb before her.

'It was the house,' she whispers. 'There was a woman

shouting, and then, I don't know, Bavar. I don't think it was me.' She looks up at me and I see how close we came to really hurting ourselves. Her eyes are streaming, and there are dark smudges on her flushed skin. 'It was the house.'

'What were you thinking?' Aoife demands, hustling us into the kitchen. 'Look at the state of you, Bavar! Explain!'

'I told you I wanted to close it,' I say.

'But did you think it through? *How* are you going to close it?'

'I don't know! Grandfather said the first thing was to find it!'

Her mouth tightens. 'And now you have found it, and nearly lost yourself to it, and you take Angel with you! Angel, who has no place in this! You find a friend and you lead her into danger and you hadn't even *thought* about how you were going to deal with that. I thought you were better than that, Bavar! If it hadn't been for the ancestors, you'd both be lost!'

'What did the ancestors do?' Angel asks, her voice small.

Aoife takes a breath, fills the kettle with water from the tap. She's wearing a plain dark dress that my mother

221

would never have worn, but the way she moves is so like her. Sometimes it's like living with her shadow. The same, but so different too. It's not a bad thing, but it hurts anyway. Like being constantly reminded of the thing you lost, that you still crave so badly. 'They saw the danger and lent you their strength,' she says. 'The rift, the house, it is all connected; it is all the same magic. It is why this place is as it is. It is how Bavar fights. It is how they saved you.'

She's so angry, I can tell from the way she swishes around the kitchen, opening drawers harder than she has to. Angel stands there with wide eyes, listening, pale now with shock, her hands trembling as she rubs at her face.

She was the one who saved me.

What was I thinking?

You were thinking you wanted an end to it all, a little voice that was hope reminds me. *You were thinking you could rid the world of the raksasa forever.*

'I have to go,' Angel says, refusing Aoife's attempts to feed her.

'You'll come back?' I ask, following her out into the hallway, loitering by the stairs.

'I'm not leaving it alone, Bavar,' she says. 'We found

the rift, and Dad had a way to close it. I'm going to find that book he had; I know where it'll be. I'm going to find it, and I'm going to use it, like *your* parents should have done before the monster came down and killed *mine*.'

And now she's said it, and it rings in the air, and it needed to be said, because we both already knew it, but it hurts anyway. It hurts more than raksasa venom.

'How do you know that's what happened?' I ask.

'I told you, on the day you fought the raksasa. They were killed by one of them. I was in the cupboard . . .' She closes her eyes, takes a breath. 'And everybody said it was a burglary, but I knew. I heard it screech, I saw it. Just like I saw you on that first day of school.'

'That's why you saw me.' I can hardly breathe. The house gets dark around me, and all I can see is her, and all her torment just flooding the air around us.

'I spent a really long time pretending I didn't believe it all,' she says. 'I'm not going back now, not for anybody. Dad was here, and your parents just sent him away, they let this happen. Is that what you're going to do too?'

'No!' I say, reaching out for her, stopping myself. 'No. I'll close it. Whatever it takes . . .'

223

She looks up at me, and that look in her eyes. Like something's wounding her, right now, right here. I take a step towards her, but she turns and runs for the door.

I feel sick.

Aoife stares as I rush away from her up the stairs and there are questions in her eyes, but I don't want to see them. I don't want to have to answer it all out loud.

It was the thing. The thing that hid in my mind, when I was poisoned by the monster. She told me, how could I have forgotten? Her parents were killed because mine got distracted. She was the girl who survived it; she was the one who saw it all happen.

Aoife said there was a child left behind.

And the child was Angel.

How did this happen? How did she end up at my school? In this house? How could she bear to be so close to it all, after everything that happened? I lurch through corridors, lights flickering all around me, until I'm in the peace and darkness of my bedroom. I can't sit still, I can't rest. I don't know what to do with myself. Everything is rushing around my head.

The raksasa killed her parents. I knew it, didn't I? Deep down, somewhere, I knew that was the thing. That was why there were shadows in her eyes; that was the thing that made her different. The thing that howled at the raksasa that night, when I thought she'd lost her mind. My parents let the barrier slip, and the raksasa escaped, and destroyed a family, and then they both fled, because they knew they couldn't come back from that. They'd gone too far into the darkness, hidden too hard from it in the parties they held every night. I remember those times so well, the lights and the heat, the smoke, the music that spiralled up the stairs and seemed to carry with it a magic that made everything dreamlike. I remember I'd fall asleep halfway down the stairs, or on the landing, my eyes heavy with the sense of it. They wove it into the air, that stillness. They used it to drown everything else out.

And then one day it was all gone. I woke in the morning and it was cold and dark, and Aoife was red-eyed, and they said goodbye, and then they were gone. They'd caught the rogue raksasa, and they'd fought with all they had, using their magic first to kill it and then to repair the barrier, and then they went, because they could no longer be trusted. It worked for a while; there *was* peace here for a while. But the barrier gradually weakened without their magic, and the rift kept growing, and the raksasa started to attack long before they thought they would, and they're still not here, and I am.

I have to end this, I tell myself, while the raksasa screeches and pounds against the barrier. I have to end it while I can, before the fight takes over, before I lose myself like they did. If there's a book that can help me to close the rift, I have to find it. Before it's too late.

Angel

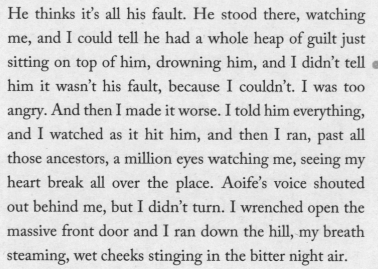

He thinks it's all his fault. He stood there, watching me, and I could tell he had a whole heap of guilt just sitting on top of him, drowning him, and I didn't tell him it wasn't his fault, because I couldn't. I was too angry. And then I made it worse. I told him everything, and I watched as it hit him, and then I ran, past all those ancestors, a million eyes watching me, seeing my heart break all over the place. Aoife's voice shouted out behind me, but I didn't turn. I wrenched open the massive front door and I ran down the hill, my breath steaming, wet cheeks stinging in the bitter night air.

Dad was there, in that house. He was there; I *saw* him. His tired blue eyes, the old hooded coat he'd had forever, that way he had of rubbing his nose when he was worried. I never thought I'd see those things again,

227

and now I wish I'd opened my eyes wider, to see it all better. I wish I'd listened harder to his voice.

I replay the scene over and over in my mind, holding on tight until the edges begin to blur and all I am left with is the sense of his fear, and my own small self, breathing hard as I sit on the narrow bed in the little vanilla house, Mika in my lap.

'I will find that book,' I tell him eventually, burrowing into the duvet. 'I will find that book and I will close that rift.'

Mika purrs, and he doesn't move all night. He curls into the space under my chin, and stays right there.

Mary's taking me shopping. She's pretty adamant about it. I want to go to the university and find Dad's book, and save the world and all that, and she wants to buy me a new winter coat.

I mean, it's not totally unreasonable. I've grown, as you do, and so the cuffs on the khaki one Mum got me a couple of years ago are a little bit on the short side. I've told Mary they're just three-quarter length, surely, and if I wear gloves it'll be fine, but no, she's insistent. She pours her cereal very firmly, and says it again: 'We're going shopping.'

'Can we do it this morning then?' I ask, fingering my spoon, looking at my upside-down self. 'And then maybe I could go out this afternoon? I wanted to go to the library . . .'

'Oh, we can do that together!' she says. 'I could do with a good book; it's been ages since I lost myself in a book.'

'Uh, well. I kind of wanted to go with a friend,' I blurt, trying to put her off.

Pretty sure she doesn't want to lose herself in *this* book.

'You mean Bavar?' Her forehead wrinkles. 'I thought you'd had a falling out. You were pretty upset last night . . .'

'Well yes . . . but we're still friends,' I say, wondering whether it's really true right now. 'And it's a really important book for, uh, history – but it's the kind you can't take out of the library; you have to read it there, with special gloves on and everything.'

'Really? That sounds interesting.'

Wow. This is tough.

'And it's the city library, not just the local one, so I need to get a train.'

The wrinkles deepen. Why did I say that?

'You seem very keen on your homework, all of a sudden.'

'I just . . . We thought it would be good, to have a little adventure.'

'I think I need to meet this Bavar,' Mary says in a firm voice. 'You can go, if he comes here first. There've been rumours about the family in that house –' she waves away my protest – 'and I'm not one to go on rumours, but still. If you want to be gallivanting around the country with him, I want to look him in the eye and get the measure of him.'

Well, good luck with that, I think.

I really hadn't planned on going with Bavar. I could do with a break from him, after everything. I feel stretched with anger, and there's no place for it to go. His parents are gone, and so are mine, and for all his sorrow he can't change what they did.

'Angel?'

'OK, I'll call him,' I say.

'He can come for lunch,' Mary says with a nod. 'And then you can go to the library.'

I mean, I could have just said I was going for a walk. I could have just not said anything and snuck out. But she was worried when I was late home last night and came in all red-eyed and prickly, and I felt bad when I saw the circles under her eyes this morning, so here I am on the 'family computer' they let me use for homework, looking up his single name and address, hoping he's got a phone number.

I've never seen a phone there. Do they even know what a phone is?

I unearth my mobile, close my eyes for a moment while a load of messages roll in from people I used to know, and then I dial.

Bavar

'You have a *phone* call.' Aoife's voice rings through the house, and second-cousin-four-times-removed Isaac gives me a wolf whistle as I head down the corridor.

I never get phone calls. Never. Not sure I've ever even heard it ring. I take the shiny white receiver from Aoife and stare at it for a moment, before holding it to my ear.

Silence.

Aoife flaps her hands at me, mouthing something. '*Say hello!*'

'Hello?' I say, turning my back on her.

'It's Angel.'

'Oh.'

Silence.

'So. About that book I was telling you about. I'm going to find it. And if you want to come with me, you'll have to come here first and meet Mary.'

'Mary?'

'My foster mother. Remember?'

'Oh.' I flinch. 'Yes.'

Sigh from the other end. 'Otherwise –' spiky voice – 'I can't go.' Her voice drops to a whisper. 'And if I can't go, you aren't going either. You don't know what you're looking for, or where it is. And we need that book, Bavar. I know we do.'

'Angel . . .'

'So –' bright voice – 'I'll see you at twelve. Come for lunch, and we'll get the train afterwards. OK?'

Lunch? And a train? My fingers go numb. I can't do those things. How can I do that? How am I going to get on a train? Will I even fit on a train? What if I bang my head when I get on and everyone notices and then they might stare, and . . .

I lean my forehead against the cool wall.

I need to close the rift. So I need to see the book.

'Bavar?'

'Yeah. OK.'

I put the phone down. Aoife is bobbing around at the bottom of the stairs. 'Was it Angel?'

'Yeah.'

'Why was she *calling* you?'

I give her a long look. She stops bobbing and glares back at me. 'I *am* your aunt, Bavar. After last night I'm not sure I want you out of my sight – I *am* in charge of your well-being.'

'Oh, that's what you call it.' I ignore the flash of outrage that crosses her face. I don't normally speak like that. I don't normally speak very much at all. 'I'm going to her house. For lunch.'

'For lunch!' Her eyes widen. 'You'll need to take something. I'll have a look; I'm sure there's something I can throw together.'

'No, it's . . .'

But she's gone.

'I like Angel,' says my mother from the little portrait by the hall table. 'She's sassy. Good for you.'

'Oh, go away,' I say, marching back to my room. The ancestors heckle as I go, and I turn on the stairs and raise my voice so it booms. 'There's an *attic*, you know. Plenty of room up there.'

Sudden silence. It's very peaceful, except for the pounding of my heart.

. . .

I'm going on a train!

Angel

'Will they even see you?' I whisper, when I answer the door.

'I don't know!'

He looks very pale and a bit sick, and like he might just walk away.

'Oh, it'll be fine,' I say, pulling at him.

He lowers his head to get through the doorway, and has to keep it a bit lowered even when he's inside. The air around him is thick and warped with his worry.

'Honestly. Just relax.'

He gives me a dark look, and hunches his shoulders.

This is going to be a complete disaster. Why did I get myself into this?

'Well, goodness. You are tall!' Mary says, as she comes towards us. Her eyes are wide with surprise.

'You must be Bavar.'

'Uh, yes. Pleased to meet you.' Bavar reaches into his coat and pulls out a lump of something covered in foil. 'My aunt made this. You don't have to eat it.'

'Not recommended then?' Mary smiles.

Bavar shrugs. I roll my eyes.

'It'll be fine,' I say, taking the package from her and heading to the kitchen, where Pete is piling a plate with sandwiches.

I wonder how quickly we can eat them.

'OK?' he asks as he turns to me.

I nod, and help him get stuff sorted on the table. Bavar comes in with Mary.

'This is Bavar!' she says, her voice bright.

'Ah, yes, of course,' Pete says, pulling out a chair. 'Come, sit. Let's eat.'

He doesn't look directly at Bavar. He sort of smiles at the space next to him, and Mary starts dishing out food as Bavar folds himself carefully into the chair next to mine.

'OK?' I whisper.

I was feeling pretty angry about everything, but it's very difficult to be cross with someone who looks as uncomfortable as he does right now. He doesn't really fit in the chair.

'Yep.'

Mary starts asking questions then in a company sort of voice, and I swear the room vibrates as he answers, but she just nods and smiles, and Pete has a bit of a dazed look on his face, but he looks happy enough too and so I suppose it's going OK, really. After a while Bavar relaxes, and Pete looks a bit less dazed, and there's even a fairly normal discussion about books for a while, and Aoife's chocolate and cherry cake is pretty good, even if it lands on the plates with a heavy splat, but still, it's a relief when it's all over.

'Now, I don't want you out late,' Mary says, looking me up and down in the new coat. I was distracted this morning so I've ended up with a mustard-yellow duvet-style thing, but it's pretty warm. 'Looks good,' she smiles. She leans in, tweaks the hood. 'Well done. I know it wasn't easy.'

I pull back. I don't know whether she's talking about shopping or lunch, or what, but Bavar is looming in the corner and he looks like he's about to start melding into the shadows, so I give her a smile and promise to be home by nine.

Bavar

She was fine, in the house.

She was OK, and then we came out, and the air changed, and I could feel her anger, and I don't know what to say. What *do* you say to someone who's angry as mirror shards coming at you? Is there anything you can say when you know why they're angry, and there's nothing you can do to change it?

And it was your fault.

Or at least, it was your parents' fault.

And now she's living in that little matchbox house with all the matchstick furniture, and now I understand the darkness in the corners of her eyes.

'Do you hate it?'

'Hate what?'

'Living there.'

She puts her hood up as hard, sleety rain begins to fall.

'I don't hate it. They're OK.'

'I'm sorry.'

'What you sorry for?'

'What happened.'

'Not your fault,' she says after a moment. Her breath steams out in front of her; she's walking too fast.

'I'm still sorry.'

'Train's leaving in about ten minutes,' she says, digging her hands into her pockets.

I can't read the expression on her face. She never looks down, never bends her head. She doesn't hide. Ever.

'Stop staring at me,' she says after a while.

'Sorry.'

'Stop being sorry.'

'OK.'

'I mean, this is supposed to be an *adventure*,' she says. 'Haven't you ever had an adventure before?'

'Not like this. Not . . . not with a train.'

She turns to me. 'Bavar, have you never been on a train?'

'No.'

239

She looks at me a long time, till I want to lower my head. But I don't. And then she grins.

'Don't stick your head out the window,' she says. 'It'll get chopped off if we go through a tunnel.'

'OK.'

Angel

The train's packed. I jump on and stand by the door, hanging on to the yellow bar, and Bavar stands on the platform as other people stream around him.

'What're you doing?' I shout.

He just looks at me.

A whistle rings out.

'Get on the train!' I let go of the bar and reach out for him. He swallows, pale and sweaty, and I grab his hand and pull and I swear the floor of the train drops as he gets on and he's breathing too fast and his head is bowed because he's too tall, he's just too *big* for it all.

'It's OK,' I say, though I'm really not sure it is.

He looks around, his eyes wild. There's nowhere to hide on a crowded train, and the people around us are looking uncomfortable. They look at me, and at the space around him, frowning. I stare back at them until they look away.

'There's no air,' he says.

'Yes, there is. Or we'd all be dead by now. Just breathe.'

What am I going to do if he passes out? He'll squash about a dozen people.

'You wanted to do this,' I say. 'Remember?'

He looks at me, his eyes all clouded with about a million worries.

'Look out the window or something; stop thinking.'

His mouth moves in a nearly-smile. After a while his grip on the post relaxes, just a little bit. The train picks up speed, rattling along, and we pass the big yellow house on the hill, and he watches it all, like he's a million miles away in his head.

'Never saw it from far away,' he says, whispering it like he's talking to himself. 'Looks small.'

I'm so busy watching him, worrying about him, that I nearly forget what we're doing, or why. I nearly forget why it's important, why my stomach is full of butterflies. I nearly forget the last time I was on a train, with Mum and Dad, heading away on holiday, suitcases bundled into the luggage racks, a packet of pretzels on the little tray, Mum with her coffee, complaining about the little lid that made it harder to drink. Looking out of the window, the sea on our left. Dad lost in a book on the other side of the aisle, until we started pelting him with pretzels. The sun setting over the water.

'Hey,' Bavar says. 'It's snowing!' He turns to me, and the light in his eyes winks out. 'Are you OK?'

I nod.

'You were with them.'

It's not a question. He knows.

'I miss them.'

'Yeah,' he says. 'I can see that.'

And he doesn't say any more. And I kind of like it, that he doesn't ask what, or why. He doesn't need to. After a while the snow comes down hard, and he watches it all like he never saw snow before, like he never saw anything before but monsters.

'How do you like the train?' I ask, after a while.

'I like it,' he says.

'Me too.'

The university looms up over us, and it's harder than I thought, to be here. I suppose I didn't really think about it that much. It's not like anything was going to stop me, and besides, I figured, it's not like I was here very often. A couple of times, when he was working at the weekend, Mum and I would come into town, meet him for lunch. That was all. But I'd forgotten how it hits you, as you walk in.

Bavar is completely transfixed. He looks like he kind of fits here. He's looking up, for the first time since I met him. I hassle him onward and end up sort of dragging him, because he can't take his eyes off all the carvings, the wide doorways, the high, vaulted ceilings. He trips up the stairs, turns as he walks, looks out of the windows to the grassed courtyard below, and generally seems to have completely forgotten why we're here.

'Up here,' I hiss at him, as he starts inspecting the portraits hung high up on the walls. 'Come on, quickly, or we'll get thrown out.'

'Will we?' His eyes snap into focus, looking a bit horrified.

'Well, we might. Come on!'

I lead the way up a narrow staircase, thankful that it's quiet. We might just get away with it. But when we get to Dad's study, there's a problem I hadn't thought about.

'Mr Duke,' reads the brass sign on the door.

I stop and breathe.

Breathe.

'What's wrong?' Bavar asks.

'Nothing.'

I knock on the door, hoping whoever Mr Duke is won't be in.

'Come!'

I take a deep breath, and open the door. He's changed it around. The desk is no longer in front of the window; it's tucked away in a dark corner. Boxes are piled along the wall, and the shelves are empty of books.

'Can I help you?' The silver-haired man frowns, standing.

'Mr Falstaff. His books.' My voice isn't working properly. I try again. 'I was looking for one of Mr Falstaff's books. This was his office.'

He leans into me. Bavar stands closer, looming over both of us.

'Aren't you a little young to be here?' Mr Duke's pale eyes squint as he looks from me to Bavar, and back again.

'Where are all of his books?'

His brow furrows. I don't want to be here any more. I don't want to explain; I don't want to see the pity in his eyes when I tell him who I am. He's going to work it out in a minute anyway; I can tell by the way he's staring at me.

'The books,' Bavar rumbles, stepping forward. 'Tell us where they are.'

There's something in his tone. Something magical, something dark and living, that warps the air and reaches out and makes Mr Duke hesitate.

'Gone,' he says, looking at the shelves, suddenly confused. 'In the library, I suppose. They always prized his words . . .' He goes and sits at the desk, runs his hands over the smooth wood. 'Yes, he was *quite* the scholar. All that travel they paid for, to find the origin of *glowing skies*, of all things. Those books of his, full of fantasy. FANTASY! And then he stumbled off into the sunset himself. Never quite believed that burglary line. He stalked danger, that man. Went all over the world just to find it! Not surprised he met a sticky end. Not surprised at all.'

I feel sick. Was *this* what Dad had to deal with? No wonder he was so desperate to find evidence in the face of jerks like this. I don't like Mr Duke. I don't think Bavar does either – he glowers at him, shadows gathering. Mr Duke stares down at his hands on the desk, still muttering to himself about fantasies, how they should have put Dad's books in the fiction section, not in occult history.

'Let's go,' I say. 'I know where the library is.'

By some miracle I manage to bustle Bavar out of there. Mr Duke's voice trails out after us: 'I don't think they'll let *children* in the library . . .'

Bavar reaches back and slams the door. The brass sign wobbles and falls off. He picks it up, looks at it for a moment, then folds it in half and wedges it under the door.

'That'll keep him busy for a while,' he muses, totally straight-faced. 'Come on. Let's get that book.'

'Bavar . . .'

'We're getting the book,' he says, standing straight, looming over everything. 'And then we're going to put a stop to it all.'

'Even if it's dangerous . . .'

'Even so,' he nods. 'If we can find this book, we can do it. That's what your dad was trying to do. We just have to see it through.'

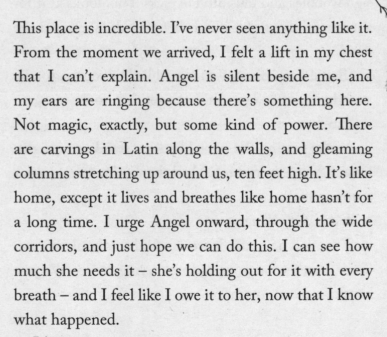

Bavar

This place is incredible. I've never seen anything like it. From the moment we arrived, I felt a lift in my chest that I can't explain. Angel is silent beside me, and my ears are ringing because there's something here. Not magic, exactly, but some kind of power. There are carvings in Latin along the walls, and gleaming columns stretching up around us, ten feet high. It's like home, except it lives and breathes like home hasn't for a long time. I urge Angel onward, through the wide corridors, and just hope we can do this. I can see how much she needs it – she's holding out for it with every breath – and I feel like I owe it to her, now that I know what happened.

It's not just me any more.

She was so quiet, as we walked through the city

streets. She moved quickly, darting down alleyways, crossing roads between stationary cars. Never seen so much traffic. So many people, all rushing along the pavements, umbrellas up, heads down. She moved between them like magic, and it was difficult to keep up. Some of the people saw me. They stared, as I tried not to collide with them, and then she turned a corner and the streets were quieter, older, the buildings golden stone rising high above us.

'Did you live here, before?'

'On the outskirts.'

'It's busy.'

'Saturday.' She shrugged. 'Shoppers, tourists . . .'

I wanted to ask if she has friends here, if she still sees them, but she was holding herself so tight that it felt like if I asked the wrong thing she might break. And I don't want her to break. I don't know how I'd fix her.

'How does the hiding thing work?' she asks now.

'Concentration,' I say. 'And other people, a bit. If they want to see me, they'll see me, no matter what I do. But most people don't really want to see things they can't explain, so it's usually easy. I just concentrate on being small.'

'Mary saw you, and Pete didn't, not really, not to start with.'

'Sometimes people want to; sometimes they don't. Mary's more curious than he is. That's all.'

'And you weren't concentrating?'

'Thought it'd be a bit strange if I turned up invisible, so I was concentrating on not concentrating . . .'

The library is enormous. A dull yellow light comes in through the windows as the sun sets, and shadows stretch between the green-shaded lights. It's quiet, only a handful of people sitting at the little dark wood desks, lamps lit over clusters of books.

The woman sitting at the curved front desk doesn't look particularly happy to be here. Angel is flitting around next to me, her fingers playing with the toggles on her coat. I think she's too nervous to go in, but she's not about to tell me that.

'I'll go in,' I whisper eventually.

'No. You won't know what you're looking for.'

'I'm guessing it'll be book shaped?'

She gestures at the millions of books lining the walls, from floor to ceiling and then up a spiral staircase to another floor. 'Go on then!'

'Well, you'll have to give me a clue, obviously.'

'*I* want to go in there and get it.'

'OK, so how are you going to do that?'

'Well, you'll have to create a diversion,' she says. I'd laugh, but her eyes are pretty sharp right now. 'Do you think you can do that?'

'What kind of diversion?'

'I don't know! Do a bit of roaring out here, or creep in and start moving books about – anything!'

'I'm not doing that. I'll just come in with you.'

'How's that going to help?'

'Maybe I can hide you too.'

She stares at me for a moment. 'Oh,' she says. 'That makes sense. Can you though? How long for?'

'I don't know. Did it before, at school.'

'But I wasn't *really* hiding then. This is different.'

'Well, do you want to try it, or do you want to stand out here all day looking like you're talking to yourself?' I ask, folding my arms.

She scowls. 'Let's just do it.'

I reach down inside myself for that feeling – that feeling of being small and insignificant. It's harder to find than usual; it's been a busy day, and my mind is distracted by all the things going on around us. I feel bigger when I'm around her. When we're out doing things.

'Any time you like.' She sighs.

I move up closer to her, extending the feeling.

'You'll have to stay close,' I say. My voice sounds like it's coming from somewhere else – everything's muffled, dark around the edges.

She moves in close to my left side. 'Come on then,' she says, and we move forward, a bit awkwardly, past the woman on the desk, who frowns and looks up. Her eyes search the air around us for a moment, then she turns her attention back to the main entrance. A couple of students arrive, diverting her, and then we're in and it's dark and kind of musty and Angel is close and warm and I get a weird, slipping feeling, but I hold on to the feeling of small and stick to the shadows, and slowly we make our way.

'Where do you think it'll be?' I ask.

'Mr Duke said something about occult history,' she says. 'I guess it'll be in the reference section . . .'

252

Angel

'You have to get in closer,' Bavar hisses, as we walk past a row of desks and lowered heads.

'This is stupid,' I mutter, squishing myself into his side. 'I mean, they probably won't even care if we're here. They probably wouldn't even *notice*.'

'Do you reckon?' He shifts next to me. His feet are enormous. I wonder where he buys his shoes. I feel like a squirrel in a tree. 'I think they'd notice you. Where's the occult section then?'

'Over here.' I pull him to the left, and we hobble down a carpeted aisle that gets darker as we go, away from the windows and barely lit by the pale globe lanterns hanging from the ceiling.

The shelves stretch in front of us, thousands, millions of books, their spines gleaming with golden words and names of people I've never heard of, and – somewhere – my father's words are here.

'Alphabetical first,' Bavar says. 'We'll find it.' He moves away, and it's suddenly colder and darker. 'Falstaff . . . Falstaff . . .'

There's a low rumble and I stare at him, as he flits about the shelves, eyes bright, fingers reaching out, touching the shelves, the books, and I realize he's humming.

'Here – F . . . Falk . . . Falstaff. Medieval mythology . . . ?'

'No.' I move closer, look up at where he's pointing. 'We're looking for Marcel – *M. Falstaff.* He's not here.'

'So –' he peers down the aisle – 'hang on. This is medieval history; you said we needed occult.'

He moves down, running his fingers along the shelves, and I follow him. There's a roaring in my ears. I don't know how I'm going to feel if we find it. I remember how he held it, when I saw him in the mirror; as though it would all be better, if only they'd just let him show them. Do I really want to know what darkness he had found, while me and Mum just got on with our normal lives? Part of me just wants to run away right now and stop it all before it gets any harder.

But I don't. I just keep following Bavar as the shelves get narrower, and the library darkens around us.

'Aha!' he bursts out, making me jump. '*History of the Occult*. Falstaff . . . Marcel Falstaff . . .'

My heart thuds, and suddenly there's movement behind us.

'May I help you?' breaks in the voice of the librarian, coming down the aisle towards us. She's got a kind face, I think, but her eyes are guarded as she looks me up and down.

'Uh, we're just looking,' I say.

'I'm afraid this isn't a public library,' she says, almost regretfully. 'You look a little young . . .'

'Bavar, find it,' I hiss, digging him in the side while I smile at the woman. 'My father worked here; I just wanted to see his books.'

'Your father?'

'Um, yes. Professor Falstaff.'

'Are you with him now?'

I stare at her. How can she not *know*?

'Um, no . . .'

And then Bavar charges past me like a spooked elephant, a heavy book in his hands.

'Run!' he shouts.

'Young man!' Her voice rings out as I join him and we scarper through the aisles. He lengthens his stride. The lights wink out one by one as we pass through the library, heads raising, eyes wide as he runs, making the floor shudder. I'm running full pelt just to keep up with him, the librarian's voice still ringing in my ears, and I really hope he got the right book, because now we're running down the library steps, and when Bavar looks back at me his whole face is alight with excitement, a stupid great big grin, cheeks flushed.

'Come on!' he calls, as shouts break the silence behind us. They really care about their books here. Bavar reaches back, grabs my hand and we fly through the courtyard, past the great golden dome, and the cold air stings and the ground is slick with icy rainwater but his feet are firm and his hand is warm and it's pretty exhilarating in all.

He'd better have the right flipping book.

Bavar

I've never run like this.

There's never been enough space, enough air to fill my lungs before. This city is as big and as scary as I feel, most of the time. It makes me small. Nothing ever makes me small.

I feel like even if I wasn't who I am, people wouldn't see me, just because there are so many of them, all of them different, all of them crowded together in this one city. Tall, golden houses rise up around us, little wrought-iron balconies beneath the windows. I try to imagine what it would be like to sit out on one of them, watching people go by. There's so much to look at.

'Bavar!'

I stop and turn, and she collides with me, breathing hard.

'The book!'

I take it out of my pocket and hold it out to her. She takes it with two hands. I hadn't realized how big it was.

'Is it the right one?'

She stares at me. 'You weren't *sure*?'

'I was mostly sure.'

Her fingers turn white around the battered leather cover.

'OK.'

'So, is it?'

'I think so,' she says, holding it to her chest.

It's getting dark around us, the streetlights glowing pink as they come on. We sit in a darkened doorway and she opens the book. The pages are heavy and warped, though they can't be that old.

Images of monsters, some of them familiar. Woodland crouched beneath angry skies. Creatures laying waste to hillside villages, smoke belching from farmlands.

Raksasa.

They're everywhere.

'It's legends,' she whispers, tracing her fingers over the small ink drawing of a hooded figure, watching

258

from the shadows as creatures fight in the sky. 'What did Mr Duke say? My dad collected them from around the world. I knew he travelled, looked into stuff – I just never knew he got this far. I never believed him when he told us all those old myths . . . they must have thought he was crazy.'

'There are raksasa all over the world?'

Did my family do that? How can I fight them all over the world?

'No,' she says, her voice sharp. 'Look.' She flicks through pages of intricate drawings, diagrams. 'There are all sorts of legends, old tales of creatures going back centuries, how different places saw them, and what they did to stop them.'

'It's happened all over the world?'

'It's happened a million times over,' she whispers, leafing through the pages.

We huddle close as it gets colder, as ice begins to form on the iron railings, and there are dark things in those pages, things I never even imagined, and then we find a new thing. Different writing, like a page from something else entirely.

'What is it?' she asks in frustration.

'It's in Latin,' I say. 'It's a spell.'

'To close the rift?'

'I think so, sort of.'

'What do you mean, Bavar?' She stares at me. '*Don't* keep things from me now. We're in this together.'

'We need an angel.' I try to smile, to make it a joke. 'And other things I don't really understand. Some kind of truth, and also salt.'

An angel's tears, it says. And then something about sacrifice, and blood.

But it can't mean her.

She's already sacrificed too much, thanks to my family.

'It's just a name,' she says. 'I mean, you're the one with all the magic. Not me.'

I nod, as she closes the book with a sigh. 'We'll figure it out. Grandfather will know some of it.'

'I thought it might be easy,' she says.

'Did you really?'

'Well, I thought it *might*.' She brightens. 'We can definitely do the salt, anyway.'

'We'll work it out,' I say. 'We have the book. The spell. That's what we came for.'

260

'Yeah.' She fingers the battered leather cover. 'We did it.'

We don't speak, as we head to the train station, and the journey home is subdued, because we *did it*. We got the book. We have it, right here, and we still don't have the answers we needed – the spell is just too dangerous. Angel is silent now, lost in her own world, and I'm heading back to mine. I put my head down and whisper the words of not being seen, and I concentrate on that and nothing else because I have to go back. Back, back, back, to where none of this is possible. They all said it wasn't possible, and I put my hope into a small girl, holding a big book, and now I feel like I've been kidding myself. What was I doing, in universities and libraries, running through wide streets, telling myself that I could make it work? Could find another way to make it all end? It is endless. The sky is amber over the house as I head up the hill and I can already hear shrieking and that's mine. That's my shriek, my business.

Fight, Bavar, they say, as I let myself in through the creaking door. You need to fight.

*

I growl as I head up the stairs to the library. I get out on to the balcony and the raksasa spirals from the sky towards me, talons stretched like blackened daggers aimed at my heart. I jump out, roaring, and land on its back, its wings beating by my ears. We fall to the ground, and half-stunned I stand and I raise my arms and I don't know whether I'm fighting the monster or myself by the end, but the strike is true and the sun rises and it's all just shadows and I'm starting to think that maybe I can do this.

I can fight.

If the alternative is to hurt her, I can just fight.

Angel

School. Home. School. Not thinking, not doing.

I didn't give up. It's just a little break. People stare harder when Bavar isn't around, so I lower my head, and wish that he were here.

He was so horrified by what was in the book. As soon as I turned the page, he shrank in on himself, the light in his eyes snuffed out. And I don't know. He muttered about angels and blood, and humanity, and something about sacrifice, but he wasn't looking at me then. He was looking at something I couldn't see.

I meant to go back to the house with him, there and then. Get his grandfather to look at the book, and work out what we were going to do. But the warp in the air around Bavar got stronger and stronger, and by the time we got off the train I could hardly see him myself.

He was just an idea, a rush of energy beside me. I held on to the book, and looked at the space where he was until my eyes watered.

'It's OK,' his voice said, from a million miles away. 'We did our best. We found the book. We did everything we could.'

'We haven't!'

But he'd already gone. He'd gone, and left me standing there alone with my father's book in my arms. Maybe I should have tried harder, but I just couldn't, not right then. I was tired, and I missed my dad, and my mum, and all I had was this stupid book, which didn't have the answers I was looking for, and I'd just had enough of it all. I stood outside the little vanilla house, and the crying came, because really all I wanted was home, and no matter what we did I would never have that back.

And it was Dad who lead them straight to our door.

Bavar

They say I'm a fool.

They want her back.

But they want Bavar the fighter too, and they can't have both.

'Here I am,' I say in the mirror, teeth sharp against my tongue. 'Just the way you wanted me. Doesn't that make you happy?'

But they don't look happy. Nobody looks happy at all.

Angel

The book is haunting me. Doesn't matter where I put it in my room, I can feel it, full of secrets and answers. I've looked at it a few times, and it makes no sense to me. I even ran it all through a translator thing on Google. Whatever it is, it's pretty heavy stuff. Heavy enough to make Bavar run away from it all.

I've read the rest of the book. Well, most of it. Some of it is very difficult to read, and some of it's just a bit gruesome. Obviously I knew that Dad had travelled a lot. He was away half the year, most years, and we'd talk on Skype, and I guess I never really thought that much about where he was, or what he was doing. History stuff, I thought. Talking to people about myths and cultural heritage.

Turns out *history stuff* meant searching the world

for monster-lore. Peru, Brazil, Thailand, Norway and Indonesia, where the pages get darker, the handwritten scribbles more frantic, and there's a lot of mention of something called the Orang-Bati, which translates as 'men with wings', and in his sketches it looks a lot like the creatures Bavar's family has been fighting for so long.

He knew they were real. He saw them for himself, in the 'boiling clouds' over the depths of the rainforest, where dark things fluttered and men whispered, in fear of the night itself. That must have been how he recognized what was happening here. And I guess that's why he thought he could help. He'd found the spell, in among the writings of those ancient Indonesian tribes. The spell that closes rifts – that could have stopped it all.

But it didn't. Bavar's parents didn't use it, and all Dad did was lead the monsters to us. And now he's gone, and so is Mum, and I could just howl with it all. I'm so *angry* with him. Why couldn't he be an accountant? Or a historian who specialized in pots? Why did he have to get himself all caught up in this? He should have just left it alone. He had a *family*.

I had a family.

I pound my fists into my pillow and it all spills out in great big heaving, choking sobs, and I wish – I *wish* I could change it. If there's going to be magic in the world, that's the kind of magic there should be. Why monsters? Why *this*?

Bavar is fighting. I can see it from the window; orange skies over the hill, shifting clouds, and the black silhouettes of the creatures he's been hiding from all his life.

I wanted him to fight. I wanted to fight with him. Now I'm just sitting here in my pyjamas, watching it all from a distance.

'It's OK,' I tell myself. 'It's OK to let it go.'

'No. No, it's not OK,' comes another, new voice. 'It's not OK to let him do something he never wanted to do, while you hide here with the thing that could stop it all.'

I look at the photo on the shelf. Mary went and got it from storage earlier in the week. I hadn't asked her to, and so I think she was a bit nervous when she handed it over. My heart thumped when I saw what it was, and I was all ready to start shouting about privacy, and how dare she, and then there they were, there *we* were,

268

standing at the top of Sugarloaf Mountain, all glowing and windblown, grins on our faces. I look like Mum. Same smile, same long, narrow nose. But my colouring, that pale wispiness, that's all from Dad.

'What would you do?' I whisper now, looking at them.

But I already know. I already know, because he already tried, and I saw him do it, in the mirror. And I might be angry with him for doing it, but it also makes me proud of him. He tried. He tried to change things for the better. Maybe it didn't work. Maybe it went horribly wrong. But he tried. And then he died, saving me. And so now there's nothing else to lose.

I shove some socks on, and my boots, grab the book from the highest shelf, and on impulse the little catapult. Then I creep down the silent, dark stairs. Mika greets me at the bottom, winds around my ankles. 'Gotta go,' I whisper, reaching down to stroke him. 'Hunting to be done.'

He grins, and I let myself out and run through the bitter night up the hill to the yellow house, where my friend is fighting, fighting, *fighting*, till he's forgotten who he is, and everything he ever wanted to be.

'Bavar!' I shout, as he strikes out again and again, the raksasa pawing the ground, shrieking as it tries to advance, every move it makes thwarted by Bavar. He turns to me, his breath coming hard and fast, dark eyes glittering. He sees me, and he doesn't.

The raksasa plunges away from him, gathering speed and taking to the air with a flap of its enormous, bat-like wings. Bavar shouts up at it with words I don't understand, and the creature wheels in the sky and turns back to us, plunging down, its red body gleaming. There's a stench of sulphur as it opens its mouth and howls at us, its amber eyes fixed on me. Bavar runs to stand before me and stretches up. A shuddering roar makes my head spin, and then he catches hold of one of its wings and casts it down with a great thud on the frozen ground. They circle each other, fury sparking in the air between them, and then he launches himself at it and there's a horrible tussle that seems to go on forever, as they fight where it is still, in the shadows. And then it stops, and Bavar turns to me, still roaring.

'Stop!' I shout, as he stalks towards me. The sky darkens above us, the air freezes without the heat of the creature's breath, and my friend is lost in shadows and all the things he feared he'd be.

He howls, his eyes wide and full of madness.

So I shoot him with the catapult.

I'm a pretty good shot with a catapult, turns out.

Bavar

The sky is dark, scattered with stars. Don't often see the stars here – more often rolling clouds and far-off fires of monster worlds. My head aches. My whole body aches. What was I doing?

'Bavar?' Angel's face looms over me.

'You shot me.'

'It was just a little stone.'

'So you stoned me.' I'm so tired. The ground is freezing, but I can't bring myself to move. The cold is soothing against the back of my head, and I know there are conversations to come, conversations I'd rather just not have. Angel frowns. 'Isn't that what they used to do in medieval times?' I ask, wondering if I can divert her.

'Not with catapults.' She hauls at me, and I sit up. 'I'm sorry. I didn't know what to do.' She looks at the catapult, and then back at me. 'You're fine now, anyway. You weren't before.'

'You made them go away,' I say, looking around. I can't remember the last time it was quiet out here. Even when they're not striking, they're there, just behind the clouds, making my blood cold. The sky is dark above us now.

'I didn't do anything,' she says. 'You fought it off.'

'There are usually more,' I say. Then I see the book in her hands. 'You brought it here?'

'We can't keep hiding from it. And you said you didn't want to be a fighter.'

That was before I knew there would be a price, and she would have to pay it. She's already paid too much for my family's mistakes.

'Maybe they sense the book,' she murmurs now, looking up at the sky. 'Maybe they don't like it. You should keep it here.'

'No, we can't do that.'

'So tell me why.'

'The book has the spell. The spell . . . I don't know. I don't really understand it. But it won't be good, Angel. There'll be consequences if we use it.'

'But you don't really know. So let's go and ask your

grandfather. Let's show him the book.'

'No.'

'Yes,' she says, standing and marching to the front door. 'Come on.'

'Angel!'

She walks up to me, her eyes bright. 'You don't frighten me, Bavar. Even your most hideous fighter self is not going to stop me from doing this, *especially* since I know you don't want to be like that. I am going to find out what this book is all about, and how we can work the spell. If you don't want to do it with me, you can just stay out here in the cold.'

She runs up the steps, and the door opens with a creak, and the ancestors call her name, and for a moment I wonder what would happen if I did just stay out here in the cold, my forehead stinging, the stars singing all around me.

And then I traipse after her, up the steps and into the huge old house where I notice nobody shouts *my* name.

'Ingrates,' I mutter as I follow her up the stairs. 'She's not staying, you know. She's just on a mission. I'm the one who's been fighting; you should all be cheering *me* along.'

274

Angel

The bust is covered in that old yellow tablecloth. I whip it off, and Bavar's grandfather blinks with a metallic clink.

'Angel! Back again! And Bavar – you're not looking so happy, my boy . . . What's that you have there?' He leans forward on his post, the light catching sudden wrinkles in his forehead as it furrows.

'A book of my dad's. It has a spell in it.'

'A spell, yes. I can feel it. Show me. SHOW me!'

I open the book, leafing through until I find the right page. Hold it up to him. His eyes glow as he reads, and Bavar goes to stand by the bookcase in the corner, looking out of the window.

'*In lacrimis angelorum,*' the deep voice rumbles. 'The tears of angels . . .'

'Don't read it out loud!' Bavar snaps.

Bronze eyes stare at him, and they have a bit of a silent stand-off, which his grandfather wins. Bavar retreats to his bookcase.

'Well, it's simple,' says the bronze, a while later, when my arms are trembling from holding the book up.

Bavar folds his arms.

'You must appear before the void, and you must give it blood, and TEARS, and your heart's truth. But there's a line here about sacrifice, which I don't quite understand . . .'

'Don't you?' asks Bavar. 'It's simple, like you say. Sacrifice. Has to be done with humanity's blood.'

'Ah, is that . . . Hold it up higher, Angel – I can't see in all this gloom! Honestly, boy –' he turns to Bavar – 'you're becoming a cliché with all this storming around. Put a light on, or something, and stop CLOUDING up the place.'

Bavar mutters something under his breath, leaning forward and turning on the desk lamp.

'Yes, I see. There's a line about complicity, partnership between the cursed and the wronged . . .'

'Between me and Angel,' Bavar says impatiently.

'And the truth of that, with the tears – must be something to do with salt – and then the blood . . .'

'Blood of the fallen,' says Bavar. 'Which is all to do with angels, and humanity . . . and it says sacrifice, so it doesn't mean a paper cut, does it? And so it's not happening.'

'But if it would close the rift forever . . .' I venture. 'And it might not mean *all* of the blood.'

'So how much?' demands Bavar. 'Because it doesn't have a quantity written there. It's a lot, and who knows how you'd stop it once you started . . .'

'Actually, I'm not sure where you've translated the fallen to Angel,' his grandfather muses. 'I suppose you're thinking the fallen is humanity . . . but even so, you could just use another human – doesn't have to be Angel here, does it?'

'Humanity *is* the fallen,' says Bavar. 'And we have one right here, who just *happens* to have gotten into all this with me, and who just *happens* to be called Angel. But it doesn't matter, because I'm not doing it. Not to anybody! Take the book, Angel. Take it and go. We'll be fine without it.'

'You're just giving up?' I lower the book.

'No. I'm going to fight.' He runs shaking hands through his hair. 'I'm going to fight, just like we always have.'

'But we have the book! We have the spell – we just need to read it!'

'I can read it just fine! Who are you willing to sacrifice, Angel? Yourself? Me? Some random *human*?'

'What other choice is there? After all this, we have to do it, Bavar!'

'No, we don't. There's another way – I'll just carry on fighting.'

'And one day you'll make a mistake, and people will die, and that won't solve anything, it won't change anything, except for the people left behind!'

'I won't let that happen,' he says. 'I swear to you, Angel. It'll never happen again.'

'So I'm supposed to just walk away, put all my faith in you? I'm not doing that, Bavar! This isn't all about you and your family. It's about me, too!'

'It should never have been about you!' he shouts, spreading his arms, the air around him moving like heatwaves. 'That's the whole point! Your family should never have been involved at all.'

'So you're saying it's all my dad's fault this has happened? That he lured out the monster, made it attack?'

'He shouldn't have been here!'

'But he was! And your parents ignored him, just like they're ignoring you now! Why are you going to just carry on like they did, when it all went so wrong?'

The lights dim, and there's a sudden hush among his ancestors. Even his grandfather is looking down at the ground.

'You should go,' Bavar says eventually. 'Just take the book and go. And forget it all. Forget you ever met me. It was a mistake for me to be at the school.'

'It wasn't! It was about the only thing you all got *right*!'

But he isn't hearing me. His eyes are dark, his face expressionless. He opens the door and I'm so confused, so angry, that I can't even put more words together. I can't keep fighting when he's already lost it.

The corridors are dark and silent, the hallway an echoing cavern, and I am burning with humiliation as they all watch me go, because I was so naïve. I really thought they wanted to change things. I thought they'd fight for this. In the end though, it's Bavar's house. He is the master here, and now I know they'll stand by him.

Even if he's making the biggest mistake in the world.

Bavar

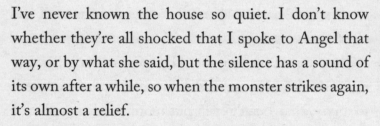

I've never known the house so quiet. I don't know whether they're all shocked that I spoke to Angel that way, or by what she said, but the silence has a sound of its own after a while, so when the monster strikes again, it's almost a relief.

'Go on then, boy,' Grandfather says, his voice solemn. 'Go and do what you said you would.'

'Did you think I should do differently?' I burst, grabbing my cloak from my father's old chair. 'You told me that I should fight, so now I am. You should be happy. Didn't you know this was the only option, really? Aoife knows it, and so does Sal . . .'

'Ah those two, they're not masters! They're here for you, Bavar, but they do not know best and they have never claimed to. These DECISIONS are *yours* to make.'

'Well, and so I made them.'

Grandfather mutters something under his breath, but I ignore it, climbing out on to the balcony and looking up into the sky. Burning bright, a turmoil of clouds and smoke and ash, and deep within, far away, the fires of that place that my family wrenched open all those years ago.

They'll never stop coming. Angel's father said in his book that it would get worse the longer the rift is open, and that's exactly what's happening. For a second I feel like I'm falling. And in that second I almost understand my parents – how overwhelming this is, how desperate it feels, and how welcome any diversion would be. Parties, new friends, old books promising answers. But none of that is real. *This* is all that's real. The raksasa, and the fight. The creature comes towards me, and I jump, and we land on the ground together, facing each other.

This is what I was born to do. It's the only thing that's left after everything else is gone. It's what I do best. The raksasa howls, its hunger for humanity fills the air, and here I am, the only thing that stands between.

Angel

It's parents' evening and I hid the letter, but Mary is pretty well connected in this town, so she knew about it anyway, and now we have to go together. It's been nearly a week since I fought with Bavar, and I've been keeping myself pretty quiet, so it's kind of a surprise to find myself out on the street, the cold biting at my nose.

I try not to look up at the big house on top of the hill, as we round the corner towards the school, but it's impossible. It looms up, dark and solitary under a jet-black sky. No raksasa tonight. Not yet, anyway.

'How do you think you're getting on?' Mary asks.

I shiver; the frost never lifted today and it crunches under our feet.

'I don't know. OK.'

'I guess OK is doing pretty well for now,' she says,

pulling her coat tighter. 'Do you like it? Do you have any friends, other than Bavar?'

'Not really. A couple of people maybe.'

It's kind of true: Grace and her little gang seem to be pretty set against me, but there are a couple of kids who I sit by in lessons who don't actually lean away from me now. They smile, say hi. Doesn't get much further than that, but I reckon that might be partly down to me. Sometimes it's hard to open up.

'Where is Bavar these days?'

'Holed up at home,' I say, my eyes flicking to the house once more. 'He's having issues.'

'Are you missing him?'

'I don't know. Maybe.'

'They're an odd family, aren't they?'

'Yeah.'

Understatement. I look at her out of the corner of my eye, trying to work out how much she knows.

'All families are odd,' she adds, shaking her head at my expression. 'I'm not about to say you shouldn't be friends; I'm glad you have each other. Just be careful. If he has things going on, you can't necessarily change them for him. All you can do is be you.'

I hunker down into my coat and march on with her,

and I can't help but notice, when my eyes stray to the house again, that the sky overhead is flickering, amber strands cutting through the clouds. They come more now, almost as if they sense he's ready for them. He'll be out there fighting soon. The urge to go and join him is strong, but I know he won't let me. I'll only make it worse. So I head on into the school, Mary beside me, and when I hear that familiar shriek I ignore it, just like everybody else does.

Though I could swear it's louder this time.

Bavar

Its amber eyes glow with rage and the need for blood, its claws rip at the stone driveway, and I need to strike. I need to do it; the world needs me to do it. But it's been an intense week, and I'm just about done in. Every night I have to fight harder to get to the same place, to beat them off before they can escape the estate, and every day I sleep, exhausted, and dream of Angel being pulled into the rift. My parents hold me back as I try to reach her, and then the words of the spell seem to unravel before my eyes as I wake.

'Get BACK,' I shout now, as the creature rears its head with a scream. I rush at it, and it retreats, but then another is swooping down to join it and together they circle me, striking with their long tails, snapping with jaws as large as I am tall. I mutter the words that

Grandfather taught me, but panic makes me tongue-tied and the spell rings hollow in my ears. I've never faced two of them together before and I'm unprepared. When I reach out for one of them, the other swipes at me from behind, sending me flying to the steps of the house.

'BAVAR!' scream the ancestors through the open door. 'GET UP!'

I scramble to my feet, chanting the words once more, waiting for the power to flood through me, waiting for the magic to be with me, but my mind is fractured, full of doubt, and the tatters of that spell wind through my words, and the raksasa can smell it. They screech, and I chase after them, my feet pounding, my heart racing, and I manage to catch one of them by the tail. It curls around to face me, snapping at the air with vicious teeth, snarling, and I reach out, striking at its neck just as the other charges full pelt towards the gate.

'No!'

The gate is torn from its hinges, and the barrier breaks with a sharp smack that takes my breath away. The creature I managed to restrain is quiet now, its essence returned to the world it came from, but the escaped raksasa takes to the skies with a victory cry.

Hot-blooded and slavering with the need for food, it's heading straight for the town.

'BAVAR!' screams the house behind me. 'BAVAR, WHAT HAVE YOU DONE?'

I roar as I tear through the remains of the gate, running as fast as I can down the hill. The town unfolds before me as I go, streets full of houses, where families are settling down for the night. Lights dance in the windows, and high up above them a shadow wheels in the sky, its form obliterating the stars.

It's hovering, I realize. I look closer. Right above the school. It's night, so the school should be empty, except it's not. Golden squares glow, and the floodlights in the field have been turned on.

It's parents' evening.

We never go. I didn't even think twice about it, but now I remember. Parents' evening. Angel will be there. Her foster mother will be there. My heart lurches as I pick up my speed, hurling myself down the hill.

What have I done?

Angel

Tables stand like little booths in the main hall, teachers talking to kids and parents, and it's super-crowded, so we can hardly move. We stand at the back of the line to see Miss Pick, my maths teacher, and Mary starts chatting with another parent. She's so easy with people. She just looks at them and smiles, and they smile back. It never fails. I wonder if it'd work so well with me. I catch sight of Grace across the room and give it a try. I'm not sure it's a very good smile, but definitely my lips are doing the right sort of shape. Grace frowns at me. Oh well. At least I tried.

I'm wondering who to try with next when a shadow flickers in the corner of my eye, outside the window, something huge. Something that screams darkness and wrongness. I shrink back as a screech rises over the murmur of voices. Mary carries on talking. Nobody heard it.

There's a bang at the window, people turn and stare for a second, but they don't seem to see the thick shadow that stalks outside; they turn away again, back to the patient queues and the teachers. I remember the first time I heard that noise. I remember how quickly it changed from something that couldn't be possible to something that changed my life forever. Glass creaks as the creature strikes again, and the lights in the hall flicker. Everything stops, and for a split second it's like everybody really *sees* it.

Shock wires through the room, faces blanche, the air rushes with a collective intake of breath, as claws screech against the window. An inhuman scream sends a shudder down my spine, makes the foundations of the school rock. There's a whimper, against the silence in the room, and then the raksasa whirls away again, gathering pace for its next hit. The lights stabilize and the queues move forward, as if nothing happened. But Mary is frowning.

'What was that?' she asks in a low voice, as if to herself. 'Did you feel that, Angel?'

She sees things. More clearly than others. My heart

lurches, panic rushes through me like electricity, and for a horrible moment I wonder if I'm going to be sick. The raksasa will come back any second, and Mary will be one of the first, because she'll run towards it. She'll see it before the others, and I know she won't just stand there while people are attacked. But I'm not letting that happen. I'm not hiding in the cupboard this time. Or in the school hall.

'I'll be back in a minute,' I tell her. 'Need the loo.'

I hurry from the room, barging past other kids and their parents. A couple of people are still looking out of the window, frowning, but they don't move.

Outside it's cold, but the air stinks of iron and sulphur. It's real. It's really happening. Somehow one of the creatures has escaped Bavar's estate. The ground quakes as it turns to me, amber eyes smouldering, and I told Bavar I would fight and I *meant* it, but it's only occurring to me now that I have no idea how to really fight one. I don't have my catapult, and even if I did I know it wouldn't help at all.

'C'mon, Angel,' I tell myself, as the creature's claws strike at the ground. I rummage through my bag, hoping my fingers are going to somehow come upon a knife, or a flare, anything they'd usually have on TV in this situation. But of course I'm just me, and it's just my school bag, so I just have books, and paper.

The book!

My fingers find the leather cover and I lift it out, my hands shaking as the creature closes in on me. I open the book and turn to the spell, and I have no idea what it will do, but the raksasa backs up a step as I start to read.

'*Qui est dominum . . .*'

'Angel, no!'

Bavar runs towards us, cloak billowing, hair standing out a mile.

'What're you doing?' he demands. 'Put that thing away!'

'No,' I say, raising the book higher, making my voice low as I start to read out again:

'*Es definitum et sanguinem . . .*'

'You don't even know what you're saying; it'll take more than just words!'

'It doesn't matter!' I fire back.

The monster roars, and Bavar rushes next to me, as Mary appears in the door.

'Angel, are you coming in here?'

'Uh, yes . . .' I look at Bavar and he waves me away.

'What's going on out here?'

'We were just talking, that's all,' I manage, as the sky lights up orange and Mary blinks, confused. I take her arm and pull her back into the school, looking desperately behind me as I go. Miss Pick says quite a lot of things about concentration and something about *pi*, but I'm not really listening, I'm watching Bavar and the monster dance around each other out there, and freaking out a bit because it's all happening right here, and everyone's just sitting here having their boring old parents' evening!

'. . . So, Angel, what do you say?' Mary's voice is insistent.

'Uh, yes. Absolutely.'

Miss Pick beams.

'How wonderful. We can begin tomorrow; I'll see you around eight.'

'What?'

Mary frowns at me. 'Miss Pick is offering you a little extra help, Angel – you should be very grateful.'

'Oh yes, I am. Thank you . . .'

I have to get out of here.

Should I be evacuating the place?

I try to picture myself standing on a table, shouting

about monsters and other-worldly dangers; the rest of the room gawking, seeing nothing, hearing nothing. Or, even worse, me standing on a table, them all listening and marching out there straight into the path of the raksasa.

No.

Mary stands, and I hurry to my feet.

'I have to go,' I say. 'I'm really sorry. Bavar needs help.'

She gives me a long look. 'I'm not going, Angel. I will see every one of your teachers, with or without you.'

'OK!'

'And you will be here at eight tomorrow morning for your extra lesson.'

'OK.'

'And we're going to have a long talk about this friendship of yours when I get home. You had better be there.'

'OK, yes – see you later!'

I run, just praying I'm in time. Because the last I saw, as Mary talked and the kids swirled around me, was Bavar being dragged into the air by one of his ankles.

Bavar

This is a nightmare.

I've managed to get up on top of the raksasa, and it's darting about the school field like a mad bull, snorting and bucking and batting its wings at me, and I should be in control by now, but we're so close to the school, and all the people, the raksasa is mad with it, straining to get away and feed. I fling myself towards the ground, landing with a stumble as it rises up and screeches, its eyes on the gold-lit windows. I mutter a few words, feel my blood begin to heat, and then Angel is there again, darting in front of me, drawing the infernal book out of her bag.

'What are you doing?'

'The spell!' she says. 'We have to try it!'

'Not now!'

'Yes, now,' she says. She turns to me and her eyes are shining. 'There are people in there, Bavar! Mary is in there. I can't just let this happen!'

'I won't let it happen!'

'It isn't only your fight,' she shouts as the raksasa lurches forward, and I run in to stop it tearing her head off. 'And you can't stop it anyway. You've tried. Your parents tried. You're not winning; you need to try another way!'

'I can do this,' I grunt, lowering my head as the creature spews hot ash into the air, my arm around its neck. 'I will do it for as long as I can.'

'But we're in the school field, Bavar! It's already too late; they're getting stronger. We need to do this!'

Claws dig into my back, and hot, sharp pain rushes through me. I try not to let it show on my face, but she sees – she sees everything. She always has.

'Bavar!'

'Let me do this,' I manage, turning and shoving at the creature, my hands against its chest as its wings crash out around my head. I duck down, bracing myself against its hot body as it strains to get past me. Its claws score into the ground as it screams, making my ears ring, and I don't know how long I can hold it off.

'If you want to try the spell, you should do it at the house. Leave me here and go!'

'I can't leave you!' She takes a step towards us, the book like a shield before her.

The raksasa screams louder and tries to take to the air, but I push harder against it, ignoring the web of pain in my back – if it gets into the sky, it'll be free to strike down again, and I don't know where it will strike. And I don't know how much fight I have left in me; already shadows are crowding around the edges of my vision.

'Go, now!' I roar, looking back at her as the creature snaps its jaws over my head, a low, guttural growl rumbling in its chest. Angel thrusts her chin out, but I can see in her eyes she knows I'm right.

'Bavar . . .'

'You have to let me do this,' I say, turning to her, still straining to keep the raksasa from getting to her. 'I let it out. I swore I never would, and it's happened already.' I feel sick at the thought. I haven't even been doing this for a year and already I've failed. 'Let me finish this while you go and start the spell. I'll be there soon . . .'

'You promise?' Her eyes dart up to the monster,

296

then back down to me. 'Bavar, you have to promise. You can't lose this one.'

'I won't,' I grunt, turning back to the monster, ignoring fresh pain in my back as it rears up again, ash falling. For a second I'm in tune with everything. I can hear the snow falling, Angel's feet pounding over the frozen ground, the murmur of conversation in the school. The moon is a bright ball in the sky, coming towards me, faster and faster as I stretch up, shadows melding all around me, and I look the creature in the eye.

I never wanted to fight. I still don't know when it will change, when the strength in me will kill the creature instead of sending it back to its world. The thought of becoming a killer is terrifying, it chills me, makes me hesitate. The monster unfurls its wings, heads into the sky. I grab one of its powerful hind legs and hang on, and we are stuck there. I'm too heavy for it to fly, and it's too strong for me to bring down.

'Run, Angel,' I whisper, as the moon winks out.

297

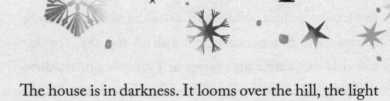

Angel

The house is in darkness. It looms over the hill, the light of the moon a pale, shadowy thing that accentuates its oddness.

I left him there.

I left him fighting a monster, with my foster mother and all those other people just yards away.

I shove the book into my bag and scramble through the hole in the gate. Twisted strands of iron clutch at my clothes, and for a moment I'm almost crying with panic, just at the thought of everything that might be happening at the school.

'*Come on, Angel,*' says my mother's voice. '*It's easy. Just one step at a time, remember?*'

'It's *not* easy,' I whisper through hot tears, finally clearing the mess of the gate and striding up the driveway. The house is quiet before me, the sense of it different somehow, like something broke along with the gate when the creature escaped.

'*You can do this,*' Dad says, deep inside, where he is with me always. '*You know you can. Bavar knows it too; he's relying on you . . .*'

I creep around the house, avoiding the main steps to the door. I don't want to face Aoife or Sal. I don't want to have to explain what I'm doing, or where Bavar is. They don't seem to have even noticed what's happening; there's no movement, no flurry of panic. I skirt to the tower at the side and grab at bunches of ivy and crevices in stone and I climb up, my legs trembling, hands already sore, hoping that somehow I'll be able to get in at the top.

It is not possible to surprise a house where all things are living.

A little gargoyle I've never noticed before starts howling as I climb over the ledge of the balcony.

'Shh!' I hiss.

'Angel-girl, it's angel-girl,' it calls in a sing-song voice. 'She's here to save the day!'

'Stop it,' I say. 'You'll wake the whole house.'

'Tis already awake, my dear,' it says with an evil little grin. 'Houses like this don't sleep while skies are glowing, and small girls fight like warriors!'

Nonsense.

I force the door open and step into the warmth of the house, glad to be away from the gargoyle and the shadows of the outside.

Mind, it's not a lot better on the inside.

'Focus, Angel,' I tell myself, marching over to the bronze plinth and whisking away the cloth.

'Angel!' booms Bavar's grandfather. 'And you brought the book – well done!'

'How do I make the spell work?' I demand. 'One of them got loose. Bavar is fighting at the school – I need to close the rift.'

'Bavar is fighting at the *school?*' His voice is suitably horrified. 'He won't forgive himself if anything happens there – he has never forgiven his parents for what they did. And that was on ME.' He sighs. 'I didn't teach his mother how to manage this place. I thought I'd live forever, that I would always be here to keep the barrier strong. She had no idea how difficult it was just to maintain it. She had no real practice in fighting the raksasa; I'd kept it all AWAY from her. She met Faolan

300

and they got caught up in the glamour of it all, the magic, even the fighting – it became a way of life. They forgot about the barrier that protected the rest of the world. And then it was too late.' He looks up at me, his eyes startled, as if he'd forgotten I was even there. 'You paid the price for that, the most terrible price. And now here you are, trying to make up for my mistakes . . .' He shakes his head. 'Read the SPELL, Angel. Read it with your whole heart, and give it everything you have. Nobody can ask more than that of any being. I only wish I could do it myself.'

'You can't,' I say, trying not to think too deeply about what he's just said. There's no time for it now. 'If I close the rift while Bavar is still fighting, the raksasa, what will happen to it?'

'Either Bavar will win, or the monster,' the bronze says. 'Without a way back to its own world the raksasa cannot simply disappear. It will be a fight to the death.' He looks at me, his eyes gleaming. 'Bavar will win. He has the strength of ten men, and the training to do it. You need not worry about that.'

'But if he kills it, if he actually kills it, then he won't be Bavar any more – he'll be all those things he never wanted to be!'

'And that will be for the best, if you cannot close the rift,' he says. 'Because if you cannot close the rift, he will spend his life fighting them. He will need to harden his heart.'

But that's his biggest fear. I look at the bronze, and I can see that his grandfather knows it too.

'I'll close it,' I say. 'If it's the last thing I do, I'll close it.'

He winks at me. 'Good luck, Angel . . .'

I run out of the door, and down the narrow steps, and there's a warp in the air all around me as I go, as the house comes alive in my wake.

'We have to do this,' I whisper, running down the corridor to the old part of the house.

'WE DO, WE DO,' echo the ancestors on the wall.

Bavar

'You want to kill things,' I say, my head pounding as I look into the raksasa's burning eyes. They're enormous, threaded through with gold veins that seem to lead me inward, so that it's hard to look away.

'And you do not? You do not eat meat?' The creature snorts dark smoke that billows out into the night air and fills my lungs, makes me cough.

'That's different . . .' I say.

'Tell me why.'

I blink, try to clear my eyes. The monster is not talking to me. It's the poison from its claws making me hear things, that's all.

'Can't you all just go back?' I ask, as we circle each other. Its black-red wings are like sails trailing out over the frozen ground, sweeping through the frost.

'Back?' It makes a move forward, its tail winding out and snapping down, missing me by inches. I step back slowly, keeping my head up. 'You opened a gateway to a place we had never known,' it says in its strange, deep, smoke-filled voice. 'Where food was plentiful, and the air was cool, and now you say no, it's not for you, you may not have it.' It darts at me, its neck stretched as it screams in frustration. 'What beast would act differently? Would you put a chicken in front of a starving wolf and curse the wolf for eating?'

'This isn't your world!' I say, dodging the blow, raising my arms to defend myself as it hits out with its claws. My back aches, my head is full of echoes, and I don't want to fight any more. 'You're not a wolf,' I say, as the claws snag on my cloak. I whirl away, dancing out of its reach. 'You have to go back! Go back now. I don't want to kill you.'

'Hah, you think you'll have the chance!' It roars, taking a great run at me. 'You're half-dead yourself, boy!'

Sounds like Grandfather, I think, as snow falls around me. I pull myself up, and the creature rears up, and everything aches, everything is cold and dark, but Angel is out there somewhere, and so there is a way. She's so sure that there's a way, so determined to change it all. The thought warms my blood and lends me strength. The creature darts at me, its jaws wide, and I duck down low, raising my arms for the last time, striking at the part of its neck that is vulnerable.

'I'm sorry,' I whisper, as the creature crumples to the ground. 'Forgive us.'

Silence. All around me, silence.

The raksasa dissolves to dust before my eyes, and it occurs to me that the school is in total darkness now. That somehow an entire evening has passed while I've been fighting this thing. The night grows thicker, shadows stretch. I look up at the moon, and over towards the house, and Angel is fighting, while I stand here just breathing. She is reading a spell that calls for sacrifice, and the barrier at the house is broken; any number of them could make their way through the rift.

So I run.

Angel

The corridors are dark, and floorboards creak under the patterned carpet as I try to find my way to the bare little room where we found the rift. The pale faces in the portraits loom out at me like moons, and they watch every move, and there's a bustle in the air of their awareness, but they do not speak. I'm fairly glad of it, since I'm trying to do all this without disturbing Aoife and Sal, but it is a bit unnerving.

Also, after a while I have to admit to myself that I'm lost. I'm lost, and time is precious. I turn to the nearest picture, of a man sitting behind the desk in the library. His dark eyes are pensive as he looks out at me.

'Which way?' I ask.

'Which way to which?' he asks in a sing-song voice.

'The room we found with the rift. You remember.

You all shouted about it. I need to find it now.'

'For humanity?'

'Yes. And for Bavar.'

He leans forward, propping his elbows on the desk.

'You will care for our boy when others see him, and he is not as they are? You will be there, when all this is over, and he is alone with shadows?'

'What do you mean?'

'We cannot speak, we cannot live without the magic that is connected to the rift,' he says. 'We will miss it, but that is not the concern. Our time is past, long ago. Bavar will lose us all, and that will be hard for him.'

'You won't speak any more?' I look around me at all the faces, all the ancestors who have called my name, who have surrounded Bavar with their love for so long. 'Even his grandfather?'

My voice is a husk, tearing through my chest as I realize the full extent of it. How can I do that to him, cut him off from all of his family, when he's already lost his parents?

'His grandfather died twenty years ago,' the man says, shaking his head. 'He is as tired as the rest of us. What is more important, Angel? You must decide!'

'Tell me the way,' I say in a low voice, steeling myself.

I'm not sure I can do it.

But I'm at least going to find the right room before I make that decision.

Bavar

Run. Run. Staggering, stumbling, slipping on ice, jumping fences, crossing frozen fields, just to get there quicker. The gate is a twist of black metal, the warped ends curving wickedly into the night. The clouds begin to boil overhead as I run up the drive, and the moon is quickly lost in fire. I keep my head low and steel myself, racing up the steps as darkness creeps in the corners of my eyes and my heart trips in my chest. My back is on fire, every move like a new strike of its claws.

'Angel,' I mutter.

'ANGEL!' shouts the house around me as the front door opens.

I can see the magic in the air now, glowing through the darkness like a thin silver cobweb that threads through every ancestor and catches at me, and sends me on with power in my veins.

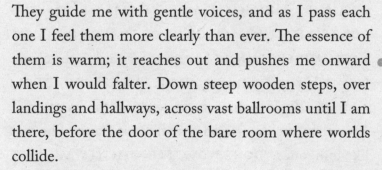

Angel

They guide me with gentle voices, and as I pass each one I feel them more clearly than ever. The essence of them is warm; it reaches out and pushes me onward when I would falter. Down steep wooden steps, over landings and hallways, across vast ballrooms until I am there, before the door of the bare room where worlds collide.

And then I stop.

Bavar will have fought the monster. He'll have sent it back to its own world; our world is safe for now. I tell myself there's no rush. I should wait for him. I can't do this alone.

'YOU AREN'T DOING IT ALONE,' says his mother from the frame next to the door.

'How could you leave him like that?'

Her shoulders raise and fall in a shrug I know so well.

'IT ISN'T FOREVER.'

'Will you come back, if I do this?'

'I DON'T KNOW,' she says. 'WE ARE NOT WHAT WE USED TO BE; WE ARE NOT THE PARENTS HE NEEDS.'

'So if I do this, he'll be alone. All the others will be gone as well.'

'THEIR LIKENESSES WILL REMAIN, IN THE PORTRAITS. THE MEMORIES OF THEIR VOICES. HE WILL UNDERSTAND.' She leans forward in the chaise longue, her eyes glittering. 'DO IT, ANGEL. DO IT FOR ALL OF US.' Her sharp teeth catch on the words, and I see then the desolation that flirts at Bavar. She was like him, once. 'DO IT NOW, BECAUSE YES, WE LEFT HIM. AND WE SHOULDN'T HAVE, BUT WE DID, AND WE CAN'T GET TO YOU FAST ENOUGH NOW. THERE'S NOTHING WE CAN DO; IT'S UP TO YOU.'

I take the book out, wrench open the door. The world blazes around me. I take the little knife and cut into my palm, and my tears are already falling as I start to speak the words, and I don't know whether I want this to work or not, but I'm doing it, and whatever happens, at least I was here. I wasn't hiding in a cupboard, too afraid to meet the demons who tore my life apart. I was here, doing everything I could to stop it from ever happening again.

Bavar

The house has dwindled to silence around me and I seem to have become lost in its maze. I tread softly, as walls melt around me, and the carpet leads me forward. I tread, and cling to walls and banisters and nooks and crannies, and I make my way through the forest that swims in my head and makes all things nonsense.

'Nonsense,' I whisper. 'It's all nonsense.'

And nobody corrects me. The portraits are quiet; the eyes of my ancestors are dark and hollow. What has happened here?

Am I too late?

The door to the room is open. The rift is wide, belching rage and flames. Angel is curled in a corner, the book open on the floor beside her.

'No,' I whisper, noticing the knife by her side.

314

She looks up.

'Didn't work,' she says, exhausted. Her hair stands out around her head in a wiry, static mess; her skin is glistening with sweat. 'I couldn't get close enough. It was too much . . .'

'We'll make it work together,' I manage, the words clumsy on my tongue as I move towards her. 'Here . . .' I use the knife, watch numbly as blood wells up, and hold my arm out to the violent, swirling rift. 'Blood, and salt, and . . .' I shake my head, frustrated. 'What was the other thing?'

'Tears of the fallen, heart's truth, or heart's pain, something,' she says.

Too much, I think numbly. I tear at the lining of my coat; wrap a strand of silk around her hand.

'Read the spell,' she whispers. 'I already did it once, but I don't know Latin – I don't know if I did it right.'

She pushes the book towards me, and the words swim before my eyes. I know it all by heart already, but there's a piece missing – I can see that now. The piece that puts it all to rest.

I am the fallen. This whole family, we are the fallen. We are the ones who opened the rift and let the creatures see a world they never would have seen. We are the ones who let them smell the blood of humanity until it was all they craved. I watch my blood spill, and Angel is silent beside me, and I hold her hand and hope my warmth is enough for both of us, just while I read this, just until I get to the end, because she looks so cold and small, and I don't know . . . I don't know how she's survived this long, with all she has seen. But there's one thing I do know. If she can, then so can I. I can do this.

The words are like fire; they hurt as they flow. I go faster, speak louder, and Angel is trying to tell me something, but her voice is a whisper, and the words I'm saying have a life of their own. Dark shapes form within the rift, screaming as they dart towards us. I raise my voice, shouting, and Angel's voice gets more insistent, and I realize she's crying, her hand pulling at mine as if to tell me something that's desperately important, but it's too late. Too late for listening, or for questions. Too late for doubts. Too late even for words. I finish the spell and it isn't enough, so I roar into the abyss, and the raksasa halt in their tracks because that is a language they understand, and it is friendship and regret and sorrow and – more than that – it is hope. It is the hope that comes out of fighting for something, knowing that you aren't fighting alone. It is Angel's

hand in mine, her voice roaring alongside mine. The
raksasa understand that. They hesitate. The magic, the
house, the rift itself and the creatures who live beyond
it – for an instant we are all together in this. We are
connected.

And then something deep inside me snaps, and
we are not. I stumble forward with a sharp cry, and
everything gets darker. The world of the raksasa begins
to fade, the temperature of the room plummets . . .

'Bavar!'

Angel's voice, bright beside me.

'Is it done?' I whisper, my head throbbing.

'You did it!'

Angel

'We did it,' he says with a ghost of a smile, looking from me to the wall where the rift used to be.

I follow his gaze, I can't quite believe it's gone. A moment ago there was a whole world there.

'How did you do it?' I ask. I don't know what he said towards the end of the spell, what he put into the words that he shouted. I don't know how he roared like that for so long, till the lights flickered and the world all went to black and white. Whatever it was, I think it might have broken him a bit. He tries to stand and ends up stumbling into me.

'Uh, sorry,' he mutters. 'M'head's spinny . . .'

'You got clawed by the raksasa.' I remember. 'Did you send it back, Bavar? Did you see it disappear?'

'Yup,' he says, leaning his head against the wall and closing his eyes.

It's so quiet now. My ears are ringing with it; I've never heard this place so silent.

Bavar opens his eyes. 'What's happened?'

I stare at him. 'What do you mean? You closed the rift . . .'

'Yes, I remember that,' he says. He frowns. 'But the silence. Why did everything stop? Why did it hurt like that?'

'I was trying to tell you,' I say, sitting next to him against the wall. My head is thumping; my hand aches where I cut it. It seemed like forever since I was in here without him, saying words I didn't understand, staring into that red-gold sky and just willing it to go away, before any more harm was done. 'You cut the magic. I think that's why it had to be you, to say the words like that. Your connection with the house, and the magic that opened the rift in the first place. That's what you got rid of.'

'I got rid of the magic? *All* of the magic? What does that even mean?'

He looks so confused, so lost. And I don't want to be the one to tell him. I don't want to be the one who pushed and pushed until this happened, but I was, and now he's lost so much.

'It means it's over,' I say. 'The rift is gone. No more raksasa. No more fighting.'

'But there's more,' he says, his eyes never leaving mine.

'I think it was the same magic that was in the house. In the portraits, and the way you could stay unseen. The way you fought . . .'

I can't say it. He stares at me until I have to look away, and I'm not going to cry, not now. So I bite my lip instead.

'The ancestors are gone,' he says.

There's a long silence.

'Grandfather?'

'I think so,' I say. 'I'm so sorry, Bavar. I was trying to tell you. I wanted to warn you, before it was too late.'

'But it *was* too late.' He sighs. 'There wasn't really a choice.'

'There was,' I say, turning back to him. 'You could have kept on being as you were. You could have fought them, just like your parents did, until it was easy, or until you lost. It would have been easier, wouldn't it? Just to ignore all this and carry on like that? But you didn't. You chose to stop it. You did the harder thing. And your mum . . .'

'My mother?'

'She spoke to me, from the portrait by the door. She *wanted* us to close the rift, Bavar, before you got like they did. I could see what it had done to her; she didn't want that for you.'

'They weren't always like that,' he says. 'It was the fighting. It got to them. I get it now. There was a moment in that fight earlier, when I was in the thick of it . . . well, you know. You saw it before, when you threw that stone at me.'

'Do you ever wonder where they are now?' I ask, ignoring the catapult reference.

'Sometimes,' he says. 'I try not to think about them too much. They left so they could fight the raksasa without distraction.' He shakes his head. 'Without me. And it was better when they'd gone, for a while, so maybe it was the right thing, but they still left me alone, with all this . . .' He tips his head back, looks up at the ceiling. 'I guess . . . I thought maybe they'd come back one day, and they'd be different. Like they were before. They never did though.'

'Maybe they will now,' I say. 'I don't know. It's going

to feel so quiet here without all the ancestors, isn't it? They've been here so long.'

'I'll live with it,' he says, his voice getting drowsy.

I wonder how much he's taking in. His skin has gone a greenish colour; I guess the raksasa venom didn't leave when we closed the rift.

'We should find Aoife—' I begin, and then as if she heard me the door bangs open and she strides in.

'What on earth are you two doing?' she demands, staring at us in our huddle on the floor. 'What is going on in this house?' She stops, and turns pale. Looks at the blank wall next to us. 'What did you do?' She gasps, holding a shaking hand out to the space where the rift gaped. 'Bavar, what did you do?'

'We closed it.' He smiles, giggling a bit.

'You closed it,' she murmurs. Her hand glides over the wall. Blue patterned paper, a few cracks near the ceiling, but otherwise intact. 'Well.' She stands there for a moment, looking down at us, her grey eyes lost. Suddenly she marches back to the door.

'SAL!' she shouts. 'SAL, come HERE!'

Her voice echoes through the corridors, in an ordinary sound-carrying way. No cackles or protests, no carping from the portraits.

'It feels odd,' she says, looking back at the wall.

'We cut the magic,' Bavar says.

'*All* of the magic?'

'Mm-hmm, think so . . .'

'Gosh,' she says, reaching up, smoothing her hair, looking from the wall to us and back again. 'Oh, my.'

'Aren't you pleased?' I ask, a bit crossly, making myself stand. 'I mean, did you *want* the raksasa here every night?'

'No, no!' she says. 'Of course I'm pleased. I'm . . . I'm astounded! I didn't think it could be done. I know Father rumbled on about it sometimes; I thought it was some sort of malformation of the bronze . . . I never considered it would be possible. What a thing!'

She looks completely frazzled.

'Well, we did it,' I say. 'It took a lot of effort, and also Bavar got clawed in the back by one of the raksasa earlier so . . .'

'*All* of the magic, you say – all gone?'

'That's what they said,' I say. 'But about Bavar . . .'

'Oh, yes – oh dear, yes,' she says, turning to him, putting her hand on his forehead. He bats her away. 'He'll be fine,' she says absently. 'We'll get him some of that potion. I suppose we'll still have *potions*, won't we?'

She stares at the wall again and frowns, and then starts pacing, her hands on her cheeks, paler than ever. 'Oh dear. Oh dear me. Oh, Sal!' she wails, as he marches into the room, pushing his glasses up, looking very put out about all the fuss.

'What happened?' he asks, peering around.

'The rift! The rift is gone,' she says. He stares at her, and the sight of him seems to calm her a bit. She takes a deep breath and shakes her head. 'It's gone, Sal. All of it. It'll be fine. It's a bit of a shock . . . We need to get Bavar some of that potion, and then . . . and then, Angel, you must tell me exactly what happened. We'll work it out. It will all be fine. Are you all right? You're rather pale!'

They both stare at me.

'It was a tricky spell,' I say with a shrug.

'The spell, of course!' she says. 'Of course it was a spell – no wonder you both look so peaky . . .'

'A spell to close the rift,' Sal says. 'Well, and we thought it couldn't be done! Well done, both of you!' His chest swells as he takes a deep, luxuriant breath. 'I thought it was rather peaceful.' He darts back out into the corridor. 'This is permanent, is it?' he asks, peering back round at us.

'Pretty sure it will be,' I say.

'Well, it'll be nice to have a bit of peace and quiet about the place,' he says, sliding his glasses back on to his nose. 'This family was very loud, sometimes. Distracting.'

'Oh, to your very important *work*, I suppose,' Aoife says with a sniff. 'I don't even know what it is you do in that study of yours.'

'General world domination,' he says, with a wicked little smile. I *think* he's joking, but honestly, I'm not sure you can ever tell with Sal. 'But for now we need to fix up these two. Where is that noxious healing potion?'

Aoife glares at him, and he sighs.

'I'll get it,' he says. He walks off, humming, as Aoife stoops to Bavar.

'All right,' she murmurs, stroking his hair back from his face with a sigh. 'You'll be all right now.'

'Will we?' he asks, his eyes dazed.

'Yes, we will,' she says. 'Once I've patched you both up. I supposed it called for blood, and sweat . . . all sorts of things . . . Very crude – these spells always are.'

'It took a lot,' I say, looking at Bavar. 'I'm sorry about the magic . . .'

'Angel!' She reaches out and squeezes my arm, her

eyes glittering. 'None of this was down to you; none of it except for the better! I'm sorry . . . I'm sorry if I was a little distracted, when I came in. I never thought I'd see the day we'd all be free of it!'

'But he's going to miss them all,' I say, biting my lip, my mind going to his grandfather, up in the library, silent now. 'Was it really the right thing to do?'

'It was Bavar's choice,' she says. 'And yours. You did it together. I don't know how.' She shakes her head with a pale smile, looking me up and down. 'You're such a small thing. Such a wisp of a girl. But you changed everything, Angel. You were his catalyst – he needed you as much as you needed him. And I don't think anyone could have done better.'

Bavar

When I wake, my back is agony.

It's been a while, apparently. Aoife flits about the bed, tidying and cajoling, trying to fill the silence in the house with conversation, but it falls flat, and I can't lift my head.

Sal comes and goes. Sometimes he shouts at me to get out and get on, and stop with all my fussing. Sometimes he sits on the bed and stares at me. Sometimes he just comes in to bicker with Aoife.

'Where's Angel?' I ask finally, when the heat has gone out of me and dust motes spin in the sunlight that streams through the window. It's so bright now in here. Without the magic.

'She came, a couple of times,' Aoife says, pausing in her rearrangement of the cushions on the settee below the window. 'She's adjusting.'

'To what?' I stare out at the fields beyond the house. There's a low mist and it adds to the silence that seems to gather tight around us now.

I can't believe I'll never hear that noise again. That shriek that tore the night in two; the flurry of wings in the air above the house.

Aoife sits, fingering the embroidery on the settee.

'It wasn't just your mission, Bavar,' she says slowly. 'She put herself into it too. She put herself into it, when there was nothing else she had the heart for. What's she going to do now?'

'Live!' I say, sitting up. 'She's going to live!'

'Well,' Aoife says, getting up and smoothing her dress with a tricksy little smile. 'What *wonderful* advice.' She fixes her eyes on mine. 'Now get up. Get up and go visit your friend – show her what that looks like.'

I bluster and scowl, and make a bit of a fuss about it all, but nobody's really taking much notice any more, so in the end I do. I get up, and dressed, and when it's dark and the stars are shining bright in the December sky, I go to her. And every step of the way I'm arguing with myself, because it's over now, and she won't want to see me. She won't want to be reminded of it all now that it's done and she's free. Why will she want that?

'She won't,' I tell myself.

'Yes, she will,' I reply, surprising myself, stomping down the hill.

Angel

Such a weird feeling. After all the adrenaline, the life or deathness of it all, just to go home – a bit pale and bloodless, but essentially whole and well – and have Mary give me a lecture, and to listen, nodding, just like I have a thousand times before, and know that it's all over.

What now?

'Angel!' Mary shakes her head, her eyes bright. 'I have *never* known a girl like you – and I've raised two, and worked with a hundred more. You're like a little spirit, slipping between my fingers. Stop it! Come away from that window and listen to what I'm saying!'

'What is it?' I ask, flinging myself down next to her. It can't really be another lecture, can it? I've just been mooching around the house all weekend, in between visits to Bavar. I didn't stay long, when I went. The house felt weird, all big and echoey, and he never really seemed to notice I was there anyway.

Would he even want to see me now?

Mary scooches closer. I think about moving away, but I don't.

'You're such a bright thing,' she says, shaking her head. 'And I don't mean in the school way, especially – I think there's probably a little work to do there – but . . . we haven't spoken much, and I don't want you to think I haven't noticed.'

'Noticed?' I look down at myself. Does it show, what happened the other day? Am I different now? 'Noticed what?'

'How hard you're trying,' she says. 'Some days are better than others, I know that, and maybe something happened with Bavar. I don't know – you've been so restless this weekend. You don't have to tell me, but I wanted you to know that I see it anyway. I see you, Angel. I see how you never stopped trying. I have no idea, with what you've been through, how that feels, but I wanted to tell you . . .'

She hesitates, her eyes glittering.

'What?'

'You're wonderful,' she says, looking me square in the eye. 'Just as you are. Whatever you do. Good days, bad days, always.'

There's a long silence. I can't look away from her. She sounds so sure. Her whole self is so sure of it.

'Do you really think that?' My voice wobbles, and I wish it wouldn't, and I wish I didn't need to ask, didn't need to hear it, but I do, so badly. After what happened, I felt so lost. I knew we'd done the right thing, but it didn't make everything right. And the cost to Bavar was more than I wanted him to pay, and so I felt like maybe I'd got it all wrong. That *I* was all wrong. That I always would be, after that night when I lost Mum and Dad.

'I know it,' she says. 'I know it, and so does Pete. And so did your parents.'

I stare at her. I can't speak. I can't breathe.

'There's work to do,' she says with a smile, as if she knows I can't bear the intensity of her love just there like that, so open, for a second longer. 'But I wanted you to know that, first.'

I look away.

Breathe.

Breathe.

And I can. I *can* breathe. I wrap my fingers around the edge of the settee. Here I am, sitting next to nice Mary, in the vanilla house, breathing.

I guess vanilla isn't the *worst* thing to be stuck with.

'OK.'

'OK?'

'OK.'

And then the doorbell rings, and I get up to answer it, and a seven-foot-tall boy walks in, looking all pale and about as out of place as I feel most of the time. And Mary shakes her head at both of us as we stand there all awkward and silent, and goes to fetch biscuits.

'OK?' I whisper eventually.

'OK,' he says.

There's a shadow of a smile on his face. I think there's probably one on mine too, as we head into the sitting room and ruin its vanilla perfection just by being there.

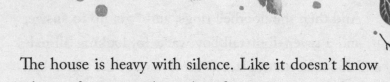

Bavar

The house is heavy with silence. Like it doesn't know what to do now, without the rift screaming at its heart.

At mine.

I guess I'll get used to it.

I miss Grandfather, the rumble and the grumble of him. I miss that tension in the air, the feeling that you could just weave your fingers and make magic of nothing. I miss all of them, even the teasing gargoyles. I kind of wish I'd taken the time to hear all their stories, before they stopped telling them. I miss all of that, but I don't miss the monsters. I don't miss the shock of their call, the score of their claws upon the walls, latching deep within my skin. I don't miss that at all.

'Bavar!' Aoife's voice rings out, and I tramp down the

stairs. She's standing there in the hallway with Angel, who looks like she's about to burst with restrained laughter, just at the sight of me. 'Your lunch!' She hands me a picnic rucksack thing, and I suppose it's an improvement on the basket, at least on the outside. She still makes the most awful, oozing cakes. Actually they're worse now. I wonder if she used the magic to make them better, before.

'You have a uniform!' Angel crows, looking me up and down, her eyes dancing.

I frown. Aoife made it for me. The usual ones didn't fit. It's pretty atrocious, to be honest. The material is too shiny, the collar on the shirt is about twice as big as it should be, and the trousers are like shapeless bags. But she meant it well.

'You reckon they'll see me now?' I ask.

'Oh, they'll definitely see you!' she says.

It doesn't sound very reassuring, somehow. I dart into the drawing room to have a quick look in the mirror. I know it doesn't really matter, what you look like, all the wise words say that. But it does sort of matter, when it sets you apart. Still too tall. Still with the beaky nose, and the ridiculous hair. But the shadows don't cling so tight now; that warp in the air is no longer there. It's a little bit brighter. A little bit more normal.

A little bit like hope.

'Ready for your first real day at school?' Angel chimes, joining me at the mirror. I can only see the top of her head reflected, she's so small.

'Not really,' I grumble, pulling at my tie.

'Stop feeling sorry for yourself,' she says, peering up and smoothing her hair. 'You wanted normal. This is normal. Worrying about what other people think of you – normal. Not fitting in – normal. Being different – normal.'

'We're both just normal then?' I demand.

'Yes,' she says. 'About as normal as extraordinary can do, anyway . . .'

There's a little shiver in the air as she says it, the chime of a piano note. The mirror mists over, just for a second, and there's a flutter of bright wings that sparkle in the morning sun.

My heart thumps. I turn to Angel. She grins back at me.

'It's still here!' she whispers.

'Not very much.'

'But a little bit.'

*

And then it's school.

Being normal.

Not normal.

Angel and I walk in together, and people stare. Boy do they stare.

We stare back.

The end.

Author's Note

The idea of Bavar was born the day I saw a boy come out of my local secondary school alone with his head bent and shoulders hunched, hiding behind his hair. The image has stayed with me ever since, and it's powerful. It reminds me of how alone we can feel, and how invisible. I wanted that boy to know I saw him. I saw him and I thought he was beautiful. I hope he isn't still hiding now, and whoever he is, whatever he's doing, I owe him a huge debt of gratitude – without him, there would be no Bavar. And as for Angel, she just came hurtling into the story, fully formed, hiding her own demons, ready for action. Without her, I suspect Bavar and I would still be feeling a bit lost. I love them both dearly.

Acknowledgements

Thank you to my agent, Amber Caraveo, for loving this story from the very start, and for all your belief in me as a writer. And thank you to my editor, Lucy Pearse, for taking such great care of Bavar and Angel, and of me too! Thank you to everybody at Macmillan Children's for everything, especially to Catherine, and to Kat, and Rachel, and to Helen Crawford-White. You are dream makers, all of you, and I am ever grateful for your faith in what I'm doing.

A very big thank you to all of my family, especially to Lee, Theia, Aubrey and Sasha, and to all of my dear friends. And thank you to the readers, authors, bloggers, reviewers, booksellers and teachers who have helped to make the last year such an incredible journey. You're all awesome.

About the Author

Amy Wilson has a background in journalism and lives in Bristol with her young family. She is a graduate of the Bath Spa MA in Creative Writing and is the author of the critically acclaimed debut novel *A Girl Called Owl*, which was nominated for the 2018 CILIP Carnegie medal.

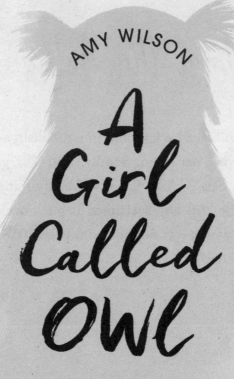

AMY WILSON

A Girl Called Owl

Owl has always wanted to know who her father is, but
when you've got a mum who won't tell you anything
and a best friend with problems of her own,
it's difficult to find time to investigate.

When Owl starts seeing strange frost patterns on her skin
and crying tears of ice, her world shifts. Could her strange
new powers be linked to the father she's never met?

'A magical debut' - *Bookseller*